When We Fall

Kendall Ryan is the *New York Times* and *USA Today* bestselling author of contemporary romance novels, including *Hard to Love*, *Unravel Me*, *Resisting Her* and the *Filthy Beautiful Lies series*.

She's a sassy, yet polite Midwestern girl with a deep love of books, and a slight addiction to lipgloss. She lives in Minneapolis with her adorable husband and two baby sons, and enjoys cooking, hiking, being active, and reading. Find out more at www.kendallryanbooks.com

When We Fall

Kendall Ryan

HARPER

This novel is entirely a work of fiction.
The names, characters and incidents portrayed in it are
the work of the author's imagination. Any resemblance to
actual persons, living or dead, events or localities is
entirely coincidental.

Harper
An imprint of HarperCollins*Publishers*
1 London Bridge Street
London SE1 9FG

www.harpercollins.co.uk

A Paperback Original 2015
1

Copyright © Kendall Ryan 2014

Kendall Ryan asserts the moral right to
be identified as the author of this work

A catalogue record for this book
is available from the British Library

ISBN: 978-0-00-813394-8

Chapter One

Knox

I knew I needed to stay calm and assess the situation, but McKenna showing up here tonight had really thrown me off. And not to mention a very pregnant Amanda waddling across my floor, groaning in pain, was putting me a little outside my comfort zone. My head was spinning like a fucking top.

Think, Knox.

I checked on McKenna again. She was sprawled across my bed where I'd laid her down, and her body was limp and pale. She was breathing, but she wasn't responding to my voice or touch. She had passed out cold from the shock of finding me in my bedroom with Amanda. I would have to deal with the repercussions later. My guess was that McKenna had driven back from her extended stay in Indiana, and finding me with Amanda in my bedroom—along with the soundtrack of Amanda's moans—had McKenna assuming the worst. Next, I tried to get Amanda to sit down and rest, but she pushed me away, insisting that walking was helping.

Knowing I was seriously out of my element, I grabbed my cell phone and dialed my neighbor, Nikki. She had a baby; surely she'd know if this was false labor or the real thing.

'Nik, yeah. Hey, my friend Amanda thinks she's going into labor, but she's not due for another several weeks—'

Nikki cut me off, saying something about a guy named Braxton Hicks and timing contractions, but before I could hear the rest, Amanda let out a bloodcurdling scream.

'I'm peeing, I think I'm peeing! Am I peeing?' She squatted on the floor, her pants growing darker with a wet stain.

What the fuck? I cursed under my breath and crossed the room to give her a hand.

Nikki, overhearing the entire thing, laughed. 'Her water just broke. Get her to the hospital. This baby's coming early.'

Christ. 'McKenna's here and passed out—I can't just leave her. And Tucker's here, too. Can you come over?'

'Sorry, I'm out of town at my mom's,' Nikki said.

'All right. Gotta go, Nik.'

'Good luck.'

I hung up the phone and helped Amanda remove her wet pants and underwear, then gave her a pair of my sweats. I'd worry about cleaning up the puddle of water on my floor later. In all the commotion, Tucker had come upstairs and was now peeking around the open doorway. 'It's okay, Tuck, you can come in.'

He ventured inside the room slowly, looking around at the two women, his eyes as big as saucers. McKenna was still out cold. 'What happened?' he asked.

'Kenna's all right, I promise. And Amanda's going to have her baby.'

Amanda let out a low moan and sat down on the bed next to McKenna. Doing the only thing I could, I picked up my phone and dialed 911. The paramedics could make sure McKenna was all right and give Amanda a lift to the hospital. While I waited for them to arrive, I sent Tucker downstairs to gather up some towels. He didn't need to be up here seeing Amanda in agonizing pain and worrying about McKenna. It wasn't healthy for his little mind to try to process all that was happening. I was having a hard enough time keeping my own stress level contained.

A few minutes later I heard sirens and ran downstairs to meet the paramedics. One man and one woman rushed inside and followed me and a wide-eyed Tucker up the stairs to my attic bedroom.

They assessed Amanda and determined that she was in active labor and got her ready for transport. Then they turned their attention to McKenna. I didn't breathe a full, deep breath until I saw her eyelids flutter and open. Her eyes met mine, and all the fear and anxiety knotting inside me relaxed just slightly.

'Hey, angel.' I leaned over her on the bed and pressed a kiss to her forehead.

'What happened?' she asked, pushing up on her elbows to sit up.

Tucker edged himself closer, nearly climbing into her lap. It seemed I wasn't the only one who'd been worried about her.

'Tuck, give her some space.'

McKenna took his hand and squeezed, showing him that she was okay.

'You came in and saw me and Amanda, and you passed out,' I explained.

Her gaze shot over to where Amanda was sitting on the sofa with the paramedics on either side of her. 'Oh my God, is she okay?'

'She's in labor. They're gonna take her to the hospital. She came here about an hour ago, complaining of a backache and contractions, and said she didn't have anywhere else to go.'

McKenna chewed on her lip, taking in the chaos across the room.

'Sir?' One of the paramedics called me over and I kissed McKenna's forehead again, then went to them.

'How is she?'

'She's doing great but progressing quickly, so we need to get going.'

Amanda grabbed my hand. 'You're coming with me, right?'

I hadn't planned on it, but the fear in her eyes pulled at something deep inside me.

'I need someone,' Amanda insisted. 'I can't do this alone. Can either you or McKenna come with me?' Her voice was shrill, bordering on hysterical.

Shit. Amanda was right. And since McKenna had just driven five hours and then had a fainting spell, I didn't particularly want to send her off to the hospital for what could very well turn into an all-night process. 'Of course I'll come.'

While the paramedics brought Amanda downstairs and loaded her into the ambulance, I explained to McKenna and Tucker that I was going to the hospital. McKenna's crystal-blue eyes turned hazy and she blinked several times, looking away.

'Will you be okay here with Tuck?' I asked her. 'The guys should be home soon.'

McKenna nodded. 'I'll be fine. And you're right, someone should be with her. We'll talk when you get back.'

Unable to stop touching McKenna, I kissed her temple and told Tucker to take good care of her, then dashed down the stairs to grab my keys. I would follow the ambulance in my Jeep.

Chapter Two

McKenna

I'd imagined the worst when I heard the feminine moans coming from behind Knox's closed bedroom door. My heart had shattered and crumbled into a million pieces as I came to the conclusion I'd lost him in the weeks I'd spent away. I'd chosen to go to Indiana and stay there while my friend Brian recovered from his car accident, but the second I heard what I thought was sex happening on the other side of that door, and that I'd lost Knox for good, I wanted to take back every moment I'd spent at Brian's bedside.

Knox being in his bedroom with a laboring Amanda was the last thing I'd expected. And I knew that said something about the level of trust I had in him. If I wanted to be here, and see where things could go with us, I needed to work on my trust issues. But one thing at a time. I swung my legs over the side of the bed and tested my weight on my shaky legs.

'Should we go downstairs?' I asked Tucker. He nodded, taking me by the arm and helping me up from the bed. 'I'm okay, buddy. I promise.'

He was so sweet and chivalrous, and just eight years old. It was an adorable combination. 'Do you want to watch the new Spiderman movie? I got it for Christmas.'

'Sure, buddy. You get it started, I'll be right down.' I wanted to throw the wet towels into the washing machine, figuring that the amniotic fluid currently soaking into the hardwood floors should be cleaned up before Knox got home.

After starting the wash, I met Tucker in the living room. He'd made a big nest of pillows on the couch for us and had the movie all cued up.

'Ready?' he asked.

I nodded.

Tucker grabbed the remote control. 'I fast-forwarded it to the best part.'

I chuckled at his efforts, not bothering to explain that I'd prefer to watch the movie from the beginning. His enthusiasm was enough. He hit PLAY and an action scene, complete with good guys and villains, played out before us. I decided it was actually rather thoughtful of him to fast-forward just to the good parts. Plus in the weeks since Christmas, I guessed he'd already watched this at least a dozen times.

I wondered how long Amanda's delivery would take and if the baby would be okay. She was delivering really early, but I knew she was well into her third trimester, so I hoped that meant the baby was developed enough to be all right. I was glad I had Tucker cuddled in my lap to distract me. Otherwise I'd probably be pacing the floor, completely stressed out and worried.

Just as the movie was ending, Jaxon and Luke arrived home.

'Hey, guys.' I whispered my greeting so as not to wake Tucker, who was softly snoring against my shoulder.

Jaxon smiled crookedly. 'You're back.'

I nodded.

'Good. Knox was like a hormonal teenager when you were gone.' Jaxon lifted Tucker from the couch and cradled his dead weight as he carried him up the stairs.

Luke sat down beside me. 'Where's Knox? Does he know you're back?'

'Yeah. It wasn't quite the reunion I was expecting, though. When I got here, our friend Amanda from group was here and she'd gone into labor. Knox took her to the hospital.' I left out the embarrassing part where I fell like a sack of stones, dropping to the floor from shock.

I knew it was wrong, but part of me wanted to grill Luke about Knox's activities while I'd been away. Had he behaved himself? Knowing he'd hooked up with someone would crush me, and since it wasn't right to use Luke's honesty against his own brother, I abstained. 'How was winter break?'

Luke shrugged. 'It was okay. I worked down at the hardware store with Knox most days, trying to build up a savings account for college. I'm going to keep working there a few days a week after school.'

I loved his determination. It made me realize that I'd taken my own education for granted. When it was time for me to go to college, all I had to do was apply, and even then I'd complained about the endless essays and applications. My parents had set aside money for years so I didn't have to worry about anything when it was time to go. As much as I tried to put myself in Luke's shoes, I knew I'd never really understand the struggles he had to endure. 'I heard you guys volunteered on Christmas,' I said.

'Yeah. It was really cool. I think we're gonna start doing that every year, make it our new family tradition. Holidays just aren't the same without our parents.'

'I know what you mean.' I loved the idea that I might have inspired their new holiday tradition.

Jaxon returned from putting Tucker to bed, and stood in front of where Luke and I sat on the couch. 'I think I'm gonna go out for a while.'

'Stay in with us,' I blurted. I didn't want to worry and wonder where Jaxon was and who he was with; I felt responsible for the boys tonight with Knox away. Maybe it was my nerves, or maybe it was because of what happened to Brian, but I'd feel a lot more comfortable with us all under one roof.

'You have to make it worth my while then.' He smirked.

'Okay?' I hadn't meant to phrase it as a question, but I was curious what he meant.

'You know how to play poker?' he asked.

'A little.' One of my college roommates had a boyfriend who was really into poker. He'd taught us both the basics.

'You have any cash on you?'

I nodded.

'Perfect. Come on.'

Luke and I rose from the couch and followed Jaxon to the dining room table. Luke tugged on my wrist, meeting my eyes with a solemn gaze. 'You don't have to play with him.'

'It's fine.'

Honestly, the distraction of a game of cards sounded better than sitting on the couch moping and waiting for Knox to get home. And I liked the idea of getting to know Luke and Jaxon a little better. I hadn't spent any quality time with just the three of us before. 'Can we play with just three players?' I asked Jaxon, settling into the chair across from him.

'Yeah, shorthanded poker. Luke, Knox, and I play this way sometimes.'

Luke rolled his eyes. 'Knox and I don't play with him anymore. He's too good. Be careful, McKenna.'

I laughed. I couldn't really see Jaxon trying to roll me for my money. I grabbed my wallet from my purse and set it on the table next to me. 'I think I can handle myself.'

Jaxon smiled at me, a devilish grin that showed off one dimple. 'I like the confidence. Game on, babe.'

Luke rolled his eyes and leaned back in his chair, folding his arms behind his head.

I watched as Jaxon pulled a roll of bills from his pocket that was several inches thick. *Whoa*. Where had he gotten that kind of money? There had to be several hundred dollars there, and as far as I knew he didn't have a job. Unless you counted breaking hearts and getting into fights. I averted my eyes from the stack of money he was shuffling through. It was his business.

Jaxon made quick work of changing my twenty-dollar bill into singles and passing the cash back to me. 'Aren't you getting in?' I asked Luke.

He shook his head. 'I don't play Jax for money anymore. Now we trade homework assignments.'

I guess that made sense. Luke was good at school and it seemed to come naturally for him. 'Oh. Well, what do you get if you win?'

A confused look twisted his features. 'I don't know. I've never won.'

I watched in awe as Jaxon shuffled and dealt the cards. The way his fingers glided over the cards with ease told me he'd spent a fair amount of time playing, a little hidden talent I'd known nothing about. It seemed the more I got to know about these boys, the more they surprised me.

'So, where is Knox anyway?' Jaxon asked, dealing the last card.

While I arranged the cards in my hand, I explained about Amanda and how her water had broken on his bedroom floor.

Jaxon made a face and shuddered. 'Nasty.' Luke's expression was more one of concern. They couldn't be more different if they tried.

I'd been dealt a decent hand—a pair of tens and a pair of sixes—and I tossed a few dollars into the center of the table. After seeing and raising, then noticing conspicuous looks from Luke, I called Jaxon and he turned over his cards for me. A full house. He took the bills from the center of the table and gave me a mocking look.

Throughout the game I continually glanced down at my phone, wondering what was happening at the hospital and when Knox would be home. I felt a little bad that I hadn't been the one to go with Amanda. I was sure she could have used a female friend there, but someone had to stay here with Tucker, and knowing the state I'd been in, it made sense that person was me. Watching Spiderman with a cuddly eight-year-old was much less stressful than being a birth coach, I was sure.

While Jaxon easily won hand after hand, Luke delivered salty snacks and cold beverages to the table, as if pretzels and chips would make up for me getting my butt kicked by Jaxon.

As it turned out, I wasn't as decent a poker player as I'd thought. Or Jaxon was just that good.

When my twenty dollars had dwindled down to two, I folded, laying my cards down on the table, then yawned. It was already after midnight. 'You know there is such a thing as letting a girl win.' I smiled sweetly, handing over more singles.

'I respect you too much to treat you like an unequal opponent,' he said, sweet as pie.

'Yeah, sure you do.' I winked.

'Let's just not tell Knox about this, okay?' Jaxon grinned, stacking his pile of newly acquired bills in front of him.

I chuckled. No doubt, Knox wouldn't be happy about Jaxon swindling me in a game of poker. 'I'm beat, guys. I think I'm gonna call it a night.'

One more quick check of my phone and still nothing from Knox. I considered calling him but decided against it. If he was helping Amanda during her labor, he'd have his hands full. Yet there was something that nagged at me. Her showing up here when she was in labor seemed a little odd to me. Maybe they'd grown closer while I was away. Pushing the thoughts aside, I rose from my seat and stretched. ''Night, guys.'

Luke and Jaxon kissed each of my cheeks and I climbed the stairs feeling happy and complete. Being near them made me feel like I was getting my second chance at a family.

Crawling into Knox's bed alone felt strange. The bed was too big, too cold, and it made me yearn for his warmth. The one bonus was that the pillowcase smelled like him. Curling onto my side, I snuggled in closer, breathing in that delicious scent, and drifted off to sleep.

When Knox finally arrived home late the next morning, I'd already made a big pancake breakfast, cleaned up, and played an epic battle of superheroes with Tucker. Knox looked weary and tired, but most of all he looked traumatized.

I rushed to his side, cupping his cheeks in my hands. 'Knox? The baby...?'

'Is fine. A little girl. Not quite five pounds. They have her in intensive care, but there's not a thing wrong with her.'

'Wow. That's great news. And Amanda?'

'She's doing well. She was a trouper. It was a long labor. For all of us.'

'What's wrong?' I took in his ragged appearance, the fine lines that seemed to have appeared overnight, and his pale skin tone. 'You look...scarred for life.' I chuckled, giving his chest a pat.

He met my eyes, deep worry etched into his honey-brown stare. 'No man should see the things I saw.'

I couldn't help but giggle again at his obvious discomfort. Giving birth was a natural process, but apparently Knox and his poor eyeballs felt differently. 'Did something...happen?'

Knox swallowed heavily. 'I just...the things I saw...I can't unsee that.' He made a face.

I gave his chest a playful shove. 'I think you'll live. Poor Amanda is the one who had to go through it all. Did she get pain medication?'

He nodded. 'Yeah. She made it a good long while without any and then it got too bad. I called the nurse, and they put something in her back that made the pain go away.'

Kendall Ryan

I smiled. Knox had proven he was a good friend and a good brother. But what I really wanted to know was if he could be a good boyfriend.

'Thanks for staying with Tucker and the guys. Everyone good?'

I nodded. 'All is fine. They were fun.' I almost told him about Jaxon taking me for twenty bucks in poker last night and immediately decided against it. I knew things were already somewhat shaky between the two of them, and didn't want to pile on any additional stress. 'I came straight here last night because I wanted to talk.'

Knox nodded, bringing a big, warm palm to my jawline and stroking my cheek. 'I know. We do need to talk, but I'm exhausted. I was up most of the night and the little sleep I did get was in a folding chair.' His rough thumb continued its path, softly rubbing my cheek. 'Can I take a rain check?'

'Of course. I guess I'll go home. Unpack. Shower. Water my sure-to-be-dead plants.'

'Okay. Thanks again for last night. I'll call you later.'

All the excitement I'd experienced when I pulled up to Knox's house last night had vanished. I still needed answers, but for now it seemed, they would have to wait.

12

Chapter Three

Knox

McKenna surprising me last night should have been a good thing. But it was more than just the situation with Amanda that was giving me pause and had me asking for a time-out today. I knew the conversation we needed to have—about McKenna's painful past and my own drunk-driving arrest. But every scenario I played out in my mind ended with her in tears and my heart broken. I just wasn't ready to go there yet. I needed her. My brothers needed her. She'd only just showed back up in our lives and I didn't want to lose her.

After greeting the guys and checking on the house, I fell into bed, drifting off to a deep sleep almost immediately. When I woke several hours later, I felt groggy and disoriented. Checking the time on my phone, I realized it was late afternoon and reluctantly crawled from bed. After a much-needed shower, I felt more alert and ventured downstairs.

Jaxon was sitting on the couch with a brand new laptop balanced across his knees.

'Where'd you get that?' I asked.

He looked up from the screen at me. 'I won some money at a hand of cards.'

I frowned. 'I told you I don't want you gambling.' Jaxon had enough bad habits without adding another to the mix.

'Relax, man. I had a good hand and I bet appropriately. It's not a big deal. And besides, I got it for Luke. I thought he could take it to college with him next year. He's gonna need a computer.'

I couldn't argue with that. Jaxon's intentions were in the right place. 'Fine. But I'm serious about the gambling.' I headed toward the kitchen before halting mid-stride to face him again. 'And don't be looking up porn on that thing. I don't want Tucker stumbling across your search history.'

Jaxon chuckled. 'That's the entire reason I shelled out six hundred bucks for this, dude.'

I shot him an angry scowl.

He laughed again, closing the laptop and setting it aside. 'I'm kidding. If I want pussy, I have three dozen contacts in my phone. All I have to do is text one of them. I'm sure you know how that works.'

My blood pressure shot up. The little shit was right. Which made me realize I should probably delete all those numbers. I didn't want McKenna finding them and getting the wrong idea. Or worse, I didn't want to chance succumbing to temptation if this thing between me and McKenna didn't work out.

'Where are the guys?' I growled.

'At the park,' Jaxon said. 'And speaking of pussy…I'm going out.' He grinned.

I rolled my eyes. Perhaps he was a lost cause. The sooner he was out on his own, the better. He would have to make his own mistakes and learn his own lessons, just as I had.

I made myself something to eat and sat alone at the kitchen table. The house was picked up and more organized, and I wondered if that had been McKenna's touch last night. There was no denying our house felt like more of a home because of her—her light, feminine scent that hung in the air long after she was gone, the sense of calm she instilled in me and the boys, the home-cooked meals she occasionally spoiled us with. God, I'd missed her.

As I ate, my mind wandered to McKenna. She'd been a vision standing in the doorway of my bedroom last night, her skin flushed and her heartbeat racing in her neck. I couldn't even imagine what she thought was going on inside my room. Finding Amanda in labor was probably the last thing she expected.

Anticipation coursed through me at the thought of seeing McKenna tonight. She had said there were some things she needed to tell me. Which meant I needed to delay pulling the skeletons out of my closet. That would have to wait. Tonight was about her.

As I cleaned up after my meal, my mind went to the events at the hospital last night. I shuddered remembering Amanda's guttural cries when she pushed the baby out, along with a rush of fluid and blood. I didn't care what anyone said; there was nothing natural about that process. It made me want to kick the ass of whoever put Amanda in that position and left her to deal with the consequences alone. He was a coward, whoever he was. Watching her hold her baby girl and sob just as hard as the tiny thing in her arms was a harrowing experience, and one I'd probably never forget. The baby was born prematurely, and though nothing major appeared wrong, she'd be under close watch for some time to come. I imagined both McKenna and I would be back at the hospital to visit both of them soon.

But right now, it was about me and McKenna.

When I picked up McKenna an hour later, she jogged down the stairs before I had the chance to go up and get her. Exiting the Jeep, I crossed around the front and met her beside the passenger door. She stood silently waiting for me to open it. But I wasn't in any sort of rush.

Taking her face in my hands, I brought her lips to mine. 'God, I missed you.' I held her close, drinking in her breath, the warmth I felt just having her near. 'When you left, I thought…'

15

'What?' she murmured, her mouth brushing against mine.

'That I'd lost you. I thought you were choosing Brian and a normal life back home over me and all my mountains of baggage.'

Her eyebrows pinched together. 'How could you think that?'

Moving my hands from her jaw to her waist, I tucked my thumbs into the back of her jeans and stroked the smooth skin of her lower back. 'That morning you left…I shouldn't have let you go like that.'

McKenna's mouth lifted in a smile just before my lips claimed hers. Not needing any more prompting, she pressed her lips to mine, running her tongue along my bottom lip until my lips parted and her tongue swept inside, gently stroking mine. What began as a sweet hello kiss turned into something much more desperate. She felt it. I felt it. This time apart hadn't been easy on either of us.

It was a damn good thing she was back. After getting a taste of how sweet and sensual she was, I knew I was ruined for all other girls. There was only McKenna.

I growled in satisfaction, a low rumble emanating from the back of my throat. 'What are you doing?'

'Distracting you,' she said, her voice breathy.

'It's working.' I pressed my hips into hers, letting her feel the hard ridge she'd inspired in my jeans. 'We should go before I get arrested for public indecency.'

She giggled. 'Where are we headed? Your place?'

I shook my head. 'I might have something planned.'

This information earned me a smile. Good, because I'd planned my very first date and something in me liked the recognition. I'd never dated, and McKenna understood what this meant.

If it were summer, I could take her to the Navy Pier and ride the Ferris wheel, or to the beach where we could sit and watch the waves of Lake Michigan crash against the shoreline. Instead, I helped her inside the warmth of my Jeep. The frigid temperatures dictated we'd be doing something indoors.

I drove us to the downtown restaurant I'd researched online. Never had I spent so much time planning a meal. But this wasn't just any meal; it was a second chance for us. Knowing it would take a small miracle to find parking even reasonably close to the restaurant, I pulled to a stop in front of the valet sign. McKenna shot me a curious glare. 'We're eating here?'

I nodded. I might not have much to offer her, but one nice meal out wasn't going to break the bank. McKenna had done so much for me and for the boys. I wanted to treat her to something special and show her how important she was to me.

After I handed my keys to the valet, we headed inside the quaint Italian restaurant, Cucina Bella, and were guided to the table I'd reserved near the fireplace. McKenna's answering smile was the only reassurance I needed. It was good to mix things up now and then.

We sipped our drinks—sparkling water with lemon for her and a draft beer for me—and made small talk. She'd hinted that there were some things she needed to talk to me about, and as insanely curious as I was, I allowed her to gather her courage without prying. When the server approached our table for a second time, I looked to McKenna. 'Shall we decide on dinner?'

She nodded.

'Just a few more minutes,' I told the apron-clad server. He turned on his heel and strode away.

After flipping open her menu, McKenna scanned the length of the page before her gaze jerked to mine. 'This place seems kind of pricey...are you sure this is okay?'

'Of course. Order whatever you'd like.' There were various cuts of steak and several types of seafood dishes.

She chewed on her lower lip. 'I can pay for myself, don't feel like you have to...'

Leaning in toward her, I placed my hand on hers. 'I brought you because I wanted to enjoy a nice night out with you. One without loud, nosy boys, video games, and stale pizza.'

McKenna's mouth pinched closed and she gave me a tight nod.

I had no idea what she was thinking, but if she was so worried about money, I could open my wallet and show her we wouldn't be locked in the kitchen washing dishes to pay for our meal. I could afford a nice dinner, for Christ's sake.

Once we had ordered, I pushed my chair closer toward her and leaned in. 'Are we going to talk about what's on your mind?'

McKenna swallowed the piece of bread she'd been absently nibbling and placed the rest on her saucer. 'Okay.'

Watching her chew on her lower lip again, I suddenly had a sinking feeling about whatever it was she was going to tell me. Like a schmuck, I'd planned a romantic date, and by the sour expression on her face, she was going to break up with me. Just my fucking luck.

'I had a moment of clarity in Indiana and realized you were right about some things.' She took a deep, fortifying breath. 'I can't keep up this pace. It's not healthy, and my parents wouldn't have wanted this for me.'

'What are you saying?'

'This is too much for me, Knox. I thought I could do it, be with you and lead Sex Addicts Anonymous, but I can't. I'm emotionally exhausted and it's not something I can continue.'

'You don't want to lead group anymore?'

She shook her head.

'And us…are you saying…'

'I feel like I probably rushed you. You were in treatment and I just…wedged myself into your life, your home…your bed.' A playful smirk lifted her mouth.

'I had no complaints.'

18

The truth was, the aspects to our physical relationship moved at a much slower pace than I was used to, but our emotional relationship was what had sent me spiraling out of control. That loving side of me had died a long time ago, on the day I'd watched my mother be lowered into the cold, hard earth. But if there was anything that gave me hope that maybe I could get that part of me back, it was McKenna.

'So you were worried about telling me you're leaving group?' I asked.

She nodded. 'And there are a few other things, too.'

'First, I'm happy that you're realizing your schedule was too full, and I think it's good you're taking a step back. Besides, my days at group are done anyway. It's no longer court appointed for me. I passed through all the sessions with flying colors.'

'Why was your therapy court appointed?' A crease in her forehead lifted her brow as she apparently realized it was something we'd never discussed.

Fuck.

'We'll get to that.' Later. *When hell froze over, hopefully.* I needed to man up and grow a pair, to tell her about my secret past, but knowing there was a chance she wouldn't be able to live with my actions, I wasn't willing to do that just yet. I wanted her to know how I felt about her first, and since the idea of telling her I loved her made my body break out in a cold sweat, I figured I needed a little time. She probably didn't realize it, but I'd never said that to a woman before. It was a big fucking deal to me and not something I just tossed around.

'Tell me what else is on your mind,' I said, my voice low and more commanding than I'd intended.

She took a deep, shuddering breath, her nerves rising to the surface. 'I finally settled all my parents' legal affairs.'

'And?' What did that have to do with us?

'I inherited some money.' She cleared her throat. 'A lot of money, in fact.' With her eyes darting up to mine, McKenna licked her lips. 'Enough to take care of college for Luke.'

I bit down and tasted blood. 'Absolutely not.'

'W-why?' she asked.

'Because the Bauers pay their own way. And your parents left that money for *you*. This is another one of your do-good charity routines and avoiding facing reality. They left that money for you and only you. They didn't set up some scholarship fund for needy kids. They wanted you to take care of yourself, have a nice, comfortable life. And I won't have you shoving this cash at Luke just to avoid that.'

McKenna drew a deep breath as anger flashed in her eyes. She could argue all she wanted, but she knew I was right. This was just another of her damn avoidance techniques. She said she'd grown during this trip home, had realized a few things; well, it was time to see if she was telling the truth. Because there was no way in fuck her parents worked hard and saved their whole lives just to see their only daughter give away their life savings to pay someone else's way while she lived like a pauper in a tiny apartment and took the bus. Fuck that. The more I thought about it, the angrier I became.

'Is this money the reason you offered to pay for dinner tonight?' I asked through clenched teeth.

McKenna lowered her eyes, her chin falling to her chest.

Great. Not only was I not good enough for her, now there was some type of financial divide between us, too. A low growl emanated inside my chest. 'Let's just go.' Feeling defeated, I reached for my wallet and tossed more than enough money down on the table to cover our bill before I stood.

She rose to her feet and followed me to the exit, her eyes still trained on the floor.

Once inside the Jeep, I tried to shake off the sting of defeat I'd experienced back there in that restaurant. I'd tried to do something nice for her, show her that she was my girl and I could take care of her, and it had all backfired in my face. She didn't trust me to pay for a simple meal, let alone take care of my own family. *Fuck*.

Noticing the way her arms were curled around her middle, I cranked the heat to high. 'Are you warm enough?'

She nodded. 'I'm fine.'

Damn it. I was being a prick. I took a deep breath, fighting to calm my raging emotions. 'Hey…' My tone softened and I reached for her hand. 'I'm sorry.'

Gazing out at the headlights of the oncoming traffic and the snowflakes floating in the night sky, I knew this wasn't her fault. Her intentions were pure, as always. And she had no way of knowing that one of my hot buttons was when people assumed I couldn't take care of the boys. It had happened numerous times over the years. I caught suspicious glares or outright accusations about how I could afford to provide for them from teachers, guidance counselors, and even my own lawyer at the custody hearing. McKenna had touched on a sore spot for me, but her involvement wasn't like the others. She wanted to help, plain and simple. And I'd all but jumped down her throat. Not that it changed my stance any, but I knew I'd overreacted.

McKenna watched the traffic pass, looking deep in thought. 'It's okay. It wasn't my place.'

I didn't say anything further, I just laced her fingers between mine and squeezed her hand in the darkness. 'You're always thinking of others. I just want to see you take care of yourself with that money.'

She nodded. 'I know. I will, I promise.'

'And I think your first priority should be buying yourself a car. I don't like you taking the city bus.'

21

She nodded again. 'I know. I've thought about that, too.'

I released a deep exhale. Good. We were getting somewhere. I knew I shouldn't have freaked out earlier and ruined the entire night. But she was still here and she was holding my hand, so maybe it wasn't completely ruined.

'I thought you'd say the first priority was me moving out of my place with Brian and getting my own apartment.'

Shaking my head, I glanced over at her. 'No. Contrary to what you might think, I like you living with him, with someone there to protect you in case of a break-in. I wouldn't want you moving out until you're ready to move in with me.'

Glancing her way, I checked for her reaction. McKenna's mouth dropped open and she stared blankly straight ahead. I might not have said the L-word yet, but judging by her reaction, that clued her in to how I felt. She wasn't just some random hookup to me. But something told me McKenna needed to hear that in words, and not just through my actions.

I parked in front of her building and brought her hand to my lips, pressing a tender kiss there before releasing it.

Chapter Four

McKenna

'Do you want to come inside?' I asked Knox as we sat in silence outside my apartment building. I might as well take advantage of the fact that Brian was out of town and I still had the apartment to myself. Plus, before our argument over money, Knox had said that tonight's date was supposed to be just us, and I wasn't ready for it to be over.

Wordlessly, Knox turned off the ignition and his dark gaze met mine, causing a warm shiver to rake across my skin. 'Brian still gone?'

I nodded. He was thinking the same thing I was—that with Brian out of town, this was one of the rare times we'd have true privacy from the boys. Delicious anticipation raced through my veins.

Knox was out of the Jeep and opening my door within seconds, causing my lips to curl up in a grin. He was every bit as eager for this reunion as I was. We still hadn't talked about the elephant in the room—our relationship—but I was trying to give him the time he needed. I'd told him I loved him, and weeks later he'd scrawled the same message to me on the frosty pane of his window. Hearing him say those words to me was what I craved, what I needed, but I was going to be patient with him. For now.

His arm curled protectively around my middle as we trekked up the two flights of stairs to my unit. Feeling his big, warm hand at my rib cage shouldn't have caused such a thrill to course through me, but it did. I was addicted to his touch more than was even remotely normal. I'd lived twenty-one years without the touch of a man, and yet right from the beginning I'd been hungry for his. My time away had only made this need inside me more acute. And Knox's thrumming pulse and barely there restraint told me he felt it, too.

My shaking hands fumbled to get the key in the lock, but once I did and the door pushed open, Knox towed me inside, slammed it closed behind us, and pressed my back against the door. The air whooshed from my lungs as my back hit the door and his solid body closed in on me. His eyes flashed on mine, dark and hungry, seconds before his eager mouth found mine.

A startled gasp escaped my throat as my body struggled to comprehend where the mild-mannered Knox of earlier had gone. He kissed me deeply, his tongue taking command of mine, his firm body pressing me harder into the door. My hips pushed back against his, seeking friction between us.

His fist twisted in my hair, angling my mouth to his as his tongue hypnotically stroked mine. Molten heat dampened my panties, my body every bit on board with where this was headed. His thigh wedged between my legs, pressing the seam of my jeans against my clit, and I let out a ragged groan, remembering our first erotic encounter began this same way. There was something naughty and taboo about being in the entryway to my apartment, as if we couldn't be bothered to take the three seconds it took to get to the bedroom.

Before I had time to process what was happening, Knox's hands were under my butt, lifting me up and spreading my thighs wide. I secured my legs around his waist so my core was positioned against his firm cock. A gush of moisture caused me to clench my legs, and I tilted my head back, exposing my throat to his exploring kisses and grazing bites.

His hot breath against my neck made me whimper and grind my hips even closer to his. Suddenly stalking away from the door, Knox carried me toward my bedroom. Gripping his shoulders as we moved down the darkened hallway, I felt my heart thrum in anticipation of what was to come next.

After tossing me none-too-gently onto the bed, Knox then dragged me by my ankles across the mattress. My heart jumped into my throat. I wanted to kiss him, to touch him, but the dark gleam in his eyes told me that he was in charge. And that thought alone caused a hot shiver to race through my veins. I liked his dominant side. Knowing I was his did insane things to me.

Unbuttoning my pants, his fingers slid into the waistband of my jeans and he tugged them down my legs, bringing my panties down with them. I squirmed on the bed, desperate to feel his rough hands against my skin, anxious for the release I knew he could give me. It had been too long; we'd both suffered too much.

'Knox…' I whimpered.

'Sit up,' he ordered coolly.

I obeyed, rising to a seated position that conveniently put me eye level with his belt buckle. Temptation spiked within me.

'Unbutton your top.'

He wanted to watch me undress myself. My fingers fumbled with the buttons on my cardigan, finally freeing the last one, and let the top fall off my shoulders. Knox found the hem of my camisole and tugged it up over my head, his fingers expertly unclasping my bra so I was left completely bare and exposed in front of him.

He leaned over me, brushing his cheek along mine. 'Beautiful,' he murmured.

With him this close I could smell the warm, musky scent of his skin. That familiar smell of warm leather and Knox sent a rush of endorphins skittering through my bloodstream. The brush of his rough cheek against my collarbone as he lowered his head hardened my nipples into points. The promise of what he could do with his mouth taunted me and I whimpered helplessly.

'Patience, sweet girl. Are you going to let me taste you this time?'

I nodded eagerly. It turned out I had no reason to be self-conscious with Knox. I had to remind myself he'd done everything and then some; nothing shocked him. I might as well go with it and enjoy the pleasure he could so expertly deliver.

Blinking up at my dark angel, I frowned. He was still fully dressed and watching me with an amused expression. Gazing down at his erection, I chewed on my lower lip. I wanted to touch him. I'd missed the solid feel of him in my hands.

'You want this?' He adjusted the rather large bulge protruding from the front of his pants.

I reached for him and unbuckled his belt, determined to push him to the same frenzied state he'd driven me to. His hands found mine and he made quick work of stripping, shoving his jeans and boxers down his hips and stepping out of them before pulling his shirt off over his head. A chiseled six-pack of rock-hard abs wasn't something I was strong enough to resist.

Need coursed through me. I wanted to touch him. Reaching one hand tentatively toward him, I paused, hesitating, before dropping my hands to my lap and looking down at the floor.

Using two fingers, Knox tipped my chin up so I'd meet his eyes. 'Let go of your shyness and insecurity. This is just me and you. And trust me, you can't possibly do anything wrong.'

I swallowed down the sudden wave of nerves and nodded. Leaning forward, I pressed my lips to the warm skin over his solid abdominal muscles, inhaling the scent of him. His muscles tightened gloriously as I trailed kisses from his navel downward. He released a helpless groan as my lips hovered just above his eager cock. Pride and happiness surged through me.

I gripped him in my right hand and stroked the smooth, velvety skin, enjoying the feel of his engorged length in my hand. Knox's head fell back as he turned his body over to the sensations. I trailed my free hand up his thigh, my fingernails grazing the fine hairs. I wished I had the skills to make him feel as out of control with desire as he made me.

Leaning forward, I opened my mouth wide, taking him in and delivering a slow, wet kiss to the head of his cock. A breath of air hissed through his teeth and I repeated the move, this time lightly cupping and squeezing his balls, the weight of them in my palm both foreign and enticing. While continuing to rub him with my hands, I moved my mouth up and down, taking him farther down my throat with each thrust.

Soon his hips were rocking forward to meet my mouth and his hands were fisting in my hair. 'Shit, angel,' he choked out, stepping back from me with a twisted expression.

I blinked up at him, trying to understand why he was stopping me. I'd just found my rhythm.

His elongated cock glistened enticingly and his chest rose and fell with each ragged breath as he fought for control. 'No more being insecure. You're fucking good at that.'

I fought off a smile, feeling oddly proud.

'Lay back,' he ordered.

I scooted up the bed and laid back, my head on the pillow, but my gaze still on him. I decided that I liked having him in my bedroom. His presence was so large and overwhelming that the soft comfort of my own space eased the experience.

He reached for his discarded pants and found his wallet, withdrew a foil packet, and tore it open. I wondered if he'd planned on us reuniting physically tonight, or if the condom was simply a remnant of his old life. Pushing the thought away, I watched him roll the condom down his length and my breathing hitched in my chest. He was big, even bigger than I remembered, yet I craved the feeling of every hard inch invading my body.

He joined me on the bed, then dragged me by my waist until I was on top of him, positioning me so I was straddling his hips, my knees on either side of his thighs. Knox's amused expression caused a smile to tug against his mouth and he rested his head against the pillows, crossing his arms behind his head.

'W-what are you doing?' I stammered.

'Giving you control. Showing you I'm yours. Do what you want, angel.'

He was giving me control? Now? Summoning my courage, I raised my hips and lifted his cock from his body, positioning the tip at my entrance. Lowering myself slowly, I felt him begin to impale me and I stiffened above him. What if I wasn't good at this?

'Take a deep breath, relax your muscles.'

I released an exhale and let myself sink down farther, savoring the feel of him stretching me, entering me so deeply.

'That's it.'

Knox might have said this time was for me, but it seemed he couldn't resist bringing his hands to my hips, his fingers gripping me tightly, biting into the skin. His face was a mask of concentration, his eyes locked on mine and his jaw tense.

'Like this?' I asked, pressing my knees into the bed so I could lift up and down on him slowly.

'Fuck, yeah, baby. Ride me. Just like that.' His voice was a rough, gravelly plea and I couldn't help but obey, rocking my hips against him over and over.

As I grew accustomed to his size, the pace built faster. I sensed a shift in Knox and soon he was no longer okay with lying back and letting me take control, he was clutching my butt and raising his hips with thrusts of his own that pushed into the very core of me.

Guiding my mouth to his with one firm hand on the back of my neck, Knox kissed me. Desperate to feel his warm lips on mine and the heat of his breath wash over me, I returned his kiss greedily. He groaned helplessly underneath me, pushing his thick cock deeper and deeper inside me with each thrust.

Without breaking our connection, his pace increased, slamming my hips down onto his lap and claiming my mouth with deep, hungry kisses. I might have been the one on top, but I was no longer in control. My body was like a rag doll being used for his pleasure, and subsequently my own. The pulsing sensation of an unexpected orgasm crashed through me, my head dropping back and a low desperate murmur clawing up my throat.

Knox growled something in response to my body's tightening and slowed his pace, his expression twisted in pleasure or agony, I couldn't be sure. 'Fuck, angel. You're so perfect.' His tight grasp on my hips loosened, as though he realized he was probably bruising my skin. I didn't care. A deep, all-consuming orgasm like that would be worth whatever bruises and soreness I had tomorrow.

Once my inner walls had finished trembling, Knox withdrew amid my protests and lifted me off of him, laying me on the bed next to him while he positioned himself above me. Keeping my legs together and my knees bent and pushed up to my chest, he held my calves in one of his hands and used his other to guide himself back inside me.

My back arched involuntarily off the bed and my hands scrambled for him, gripping his thighs as he rocked forward again and again, pummeling me with long, purposeful strokes. I clung to him desperately while he worked himself inside me, pumping his hips and keeping my legs in place.

He bit out a string of curse words and I felt the moment he gave in, his body jerking and his cock swelling inside me, filling the condom he wore.

Knox released his hold on my legs and pressed a soft kiss to my mouth. He got up just long enough to remove the condom and grab me a handful of tissues, wiping between my legs carefully before returning to the bathroom to dispose of it all. I made a mental note to take the trash out before Brian got back. I didn't need him seeing the evidence that my virginity was indeed gone and make some comment about it.

Knox crawled into bed beside me, pulling the quilt that was folded at the foot of my bed up and over us.

'You're trembling,' he whispered, brushing the hair back from my face.

I nodded. 'That was intense.'

He smiled and pulled me closer, tucking me against his side and draping a heavy arm over me. 'This feels so good, holding you like this.'

Panting to catch my breath, I curled onto my side and let him hold me. His big, warm palms smoothed up and down my body, lightly stroking me and soothing me until all my muscles were relaxed and I felt sleepy.

As I dozed off into a light sleep, feeling complete and happy, I made mental notes of all the things I needed to do. Check on Brian. Check on Amanda and her baby. And find a way to become an anonymous donor for a college scholarship and be sure that Luke was the recipient. But for now, I just relaxed and let Knox hold me snugly in his arms.

The way he'd been himself—so uninhibited and fierce, taking me over the edge with each punishing stroke—was the sexiest thing I'd ever seen. He'd claimed my mouth with deep, hungry kisses, seeking love, acceptance, and belonging. He might not have said the actual words yet, but it was only a matter of time. I felt his love in each kiss and whispered compliment.

He kissed me once more on the forehead and then rose from the bed. 'I need to get home to check on the guys.'

I nodded and got up, pulling on the pink bathrobe hanging on the back of my door.

Knox stepped into his jeans and tugged his shirt on over his head. Once he was dressed, he pulled me into his arms, lifting my mouth to his and looking deep into my eyes. I didn't know what he was trying to tell me, but I felt his love and concern all the same.

But he had told me he'd loved me, hadn't he? Not in words, but with his body. The tender way he'd made love to me for my first time, his protectiveness over me, the way he read my body and gave me exactly what it needed. It was closer to love than anything I'd had before.

'Thank you for the date tonight,' I whispered against his lips. I'd felt so cherished and thoroughly cared for that I wanted to tell him I loved him, too, but I didn't. I just pressed my mouth to his and felt his lips curl in a smile.

'Thank you for everything. For staying with the boys last night. For giving me time. For being you. I don't even want to think what my life would be like without you.'

I knew just what he meant. We were good for each other, plain and simple. Knox pushed me out of my comfort zone and made me believe I was worth something. And I forced him to deal with the pain in his past and examine the damaging coping mechanisms he employed. My life felt fuller and more meaningful than it had in years.

'I'll come by tomorrow night after work,' I murmured.

He nodded. 'See you then.'

After walking him out and locking up, I fell into bed, my body heavy and relaxed, and let sleep pull me under.

Chapter Five

McKenna

The following morning I was up early, feeling eager to jump into my new life. Of course I had my job at the counseling center and my obligations volunteering, but I was also firm on keeping some of the resolutions I'd made myself and Knox. Beginning with putting myself first. I made an appointment at my gynecologist's office for later that morning and then drove to a local salon, one of the benefits of still having the rental car. I knew I needed to return it and think about my long-term plans for transportation, but something about having a car in the city felt so decadent after surviving for so long without one.

After getting my hair cut, colored with caramel highlights, and styled into flowing waves, I couldn't stop touching it and stealing glances at myself in the rearview mirror as I drove. My hair felt so much softer with all the spilt ends cut off. It had taken nearly three hours at the salon, and while that normally would have made me feel guilty and like it was a waste of time and money, today it felt like therapy—something I was supposed to do to take care of myself. I decided my mom would be thrilled seeing me happy like this. All these years I'd told myself I should keep up my punishing schedule for them, to make sure their deaths were not for nothing. But today, for the first time, I realized both of my parents would have hated the girl I'd become. They would have hated seeing me spent and exhausted, the dark circles under my eyes. I never knew indulging myself could feel so good.

When I arrived at the doctor's office, I fought off the wave of nerves I experienced walking into the waiting room. I was a twenty-one-year-old woman who needed birth control. This might have been new and scary for me, but I reminded myself that the doctor had probably seen and heard it all before.

After filling out a stack of forms, a nurse called my name and brought me back to an exam room, where she took my weight and blood pressure, and then asked me to strip completely and dress in a paper robe and wait for the doctor.

I did as instructed, folding my bra and panties and hiding them under my folded jeans, then climbed up onto the exam table, arranging the stiff robe around me.

The doctor knocked once and entered. She was tall and gorgeous with honey-colored skin and long, dark hair. She could have been Beyoncé's sister, and I felt self-conscious sitting there in my paper outfit. But she immediately put me at ease, explaining that she'd conduct a vaginal exam and Pap smear, and then we'd talk about birth control options.

I leaned back on the table and placed my feet in the stirrups where she directed.

After several seconds and a little pinch, she stood up and removed her gloves. 'You look very healthy.'

I didn't know what a doctor might say while looking at my lady parts, but I supposed healthy was the best thing.

'What kind of protection are you using today?' she asked.

'Condoms.'

'Are you in a monogamous relationship?'

'Yes.' I nodded. I felt confident for the first time since Knox and I had begun seeing each other that this statement was true. I didn't know if it was possible to be completely cured from sex addiction, or if he still had occasional dark thoughts or struggles, but I felt certain I was the only woman in his bed and in his arms these days.

We discussed the birth control patch, pills, and the shot. I decided to go with the shot, knowing it lasted for three months and wouldn't be something I had to think about every day. The nurse came in and administered the shot, then I redressed and left, feeling confident and in control of my life for the first time in a long time.

After working my shift at the teen center, I drove to Knox's place around dinnertime. The boys were gathered around the table, eating when I arrived, and Knox set out an extra plate for me, loading it up with a piece of chicken and potatoes. I loved being here with them and as I ate, I enjoyed their banter. The noise volume was a sharp contrast to my own quiet apartment.

Knox
While we ate, my gaze kept wandering over to McKenna. Last night had been incredible. It had started a little rocky when she'd brought up wanting to give away her inheritance to fund Luke's education, but it had ended perfectly. Watching McKenna's confidence grow as she moved above me in bed had been life changing. It had broken something inside me and as worried as I was about admitting my drunk-driving arrest to her, I had to believe that all this would work out.

'Stop playing with your chicken and eat, Tuck.' I shot my youngest brother a warning glare. The chicken leg I'd put on his plate was currently performing a can-can dance.

Tucker giggled, glancing up at McKenna, and took a big bite. The little shit. He was flirting with her. She choked on a laugh of her own, covering her mouth with the napkin.

'Have you filled out your applications yet?' I asked Luke.

He set down his fork, a serious crease between his brows. 'What's the point, Knox? We can't afford it.'

I squeezed my fists at my sides. 'Get your damn applications filled out and turned in. I told you I'd worry about the expenses.' Luke needed to do his part and I would figure out a way to do mine, damn it. I was tired of them all doubting me.

McKenna stared down at her plate, looking deep in thought.

Shit. I was being selfish. McKenna had the money—she wanted to help—and my own insecurities were holding Luke back. This wasn't about me and my damn ego. Besides, I knew I had bigger things to worry about. My future with McKenna still hung in the balance, if I was being honest with myself. Pushing my plate away, I realized it was time to open up.

After we'd finished dinner and cleaned up, McKenna followed Tucker upstairs, promising to play superheroes with him before it was time for lights out. It gave me a chance to think about how to put into words what I needed to tell her.

Luke sat at the table with Jaxon's new laptop, unhappy but filling out his college applications. Jaxon had left, saying he was going out for a couple of hours. It was a school night but he was eighteen now; it wasn't like there was a lot I could do. As long as he was going to school and getting good grades, I didn't really care.

I found McKenna perched beside Tucker's bed. The bedside lamp glowed softly, illuminating a beautiful sight—a peacefully sleeping little boy, and a woman I adored tucking the blankets securely around him. My heart swelled watching her. Tucker might not know a mother's love, but I was thankful he had McKenna.

Sensing my presence, she glanced back at the doorway and spotted me. I crossed the room toward them and kissed Tucker's forehead. ''Night, buddy,' I whispered. I reached for McKenna's hand and pressed a kiss to the back of it before pulling her up to stand.

Without releasing my hold on her hand, I led her up the stairs to my bedroom. 'How many books did he make you read him this time?' I asked.

'None, actually. He just wanted to talk.'

That was interesting. What could my eight-year-old brother want to talk to her about? I followed her to the edge of the bed and sat down beside her. 'What about?'

'He asked if you and I were going to get married and if I'd be his mommy.'

Holy shit. 'What did you say?'

Her gaze met mine. 'I told him the truth. That I didn't know, but I would always be there if he needed me.'

I nodded thoughtfully and released a sigh.

'What else could I have said? We haven't talked about us since I've been back.'

It had only been a few days, but she was right. It was an overdue conversation. Still, she was putting me on the spot and she knew it. Her hands were clasped together and her knee was bouncing up and down with nerves. McKenna putting me on the spot took guts; I'd give her that. And I wanted to talk about all this, I really did, I just thought I'd have more time to plan out what I wanted to say. I still had no fucking clue how she'd react to my drunk-driving conviction.

'I've told you how I felt,' she continued. 'I've been very open with you.'

Taking a deep breath, I settled my nerves. I laced her fingers between mine and kissed her temple. 'I know. And I shouldn't have let you leave last time without telling you how I felt. There are things I want to tell you, things I need to say… Fuck.' I tore my hands through my hair, fighting for the right words. Why was this so damn hard for me? It was just as hard telling her about my arrest as it had been telling her about my past with sex. I didn't want to lose her. Couldn't.

McKenna rose from the bed and paced the room, seeming to draw strength and determination with each step she took. 'When I met you, I figured you were some sex-loving player, a guy always on the prowl, just looking to hook up with whatever willing girl crossed your path.'

I winced; she wasn't far off the mark.

Stopping at the end of the room to turn around, she continued marching past me. 'But then I got to know you—and the boys—and I realized that you weren't that guy. I discovered you were this broken man looking for love and affection, but going about it entirely the wrong way.'

She turned again on her heel, looking deep in thought.

Where was she going with all this? I wanted to tell her that loving part of me died. I wouldn't even know how to get him back, but I knew she was right.

'McKenna, let me say a few things.' I rose to my feet, facing her.

'No. You can't control everything all the time, Knox. Love is fucking scary. It's an unstoppable wave that has the power to pull you under and drown you completely. You don't always choose it, it develops, slowly at first or sometimes all at once. And other times it's ripped from your life way too soon. Like with your mom. My parents. But that doesn't mean we can give up. Love is the most beautiful thing in the world. We all deserve it. And when we lose it, we deserve a second chance. And a third. Give it a chance.'

A slow smile uncurled on my lips. 'You just swore. That was your first curse word. We need to celebrate.' I grinned at her and she swatted my chest, giving it a playful smack. 'I love you, McKenna. With every part of my heart. And you're wrong, it doesn't just scare me, it fucking terrifies me. The thought of losing you...' I shuddered involuntarily, knowing that was a very real possibility once I told her the truth. 'I love everything about you—your giving nature, your outlook on life, the way you are with my brothers.

Your heart's too damn big and you're way too good for someone like me, but as long as you want me, I'm never letting you go.'

Unshed tears shimmered in her eyes as she looked up at me.

My thumb swiped against her bottom lip as I cupped her face in my hands. 'I love you, angel,' I repeated.

Blinking back tears, she drew a shuddering breath. 'I love you, too.'

'I should have told you sooner. Did you see my note on the window that morning before you left?'

She nodded, confirming she had.

'Why didn't you say anything?'

Her shoulder lifted in a shrug. 'I don't know. For being a man with dominant tendencies, you sure know how to keep a girl in suspense. I guess I didn't want to take the lead in that aspect of our relationship. It was important to me to hear you say it.'

I nodded. She was right. Again. Christ, when was I going to learn? 'So you like it when I take control?'

She licked her lips and nodded.

I chuckled low under my breath, unable to hold it in. This girl was perfect for me. 'C'mere, angel.' I lifted her face to mine and kissed her deeply.

McKenna responded immediately, her arms winding around my back and her hands wandering under my shirt.

'Slow down,' I whispered against her ear. 'There's still more we should talk about.'

'There is?' she asked, gazing up at me with a crease lining her forehead.

Shit. I might have been tough in other aspects of my life, but I wasn't brave enough for this shit. I couldn't rip apart a relationship I was just building with her. 'I like your hair. Is it different?' I said finally, running my fingers through the long, silky locks.

She laughed out loud, tipping her head back. 'I was waiting for you to notice.'

'You're always beautiful.'

She beamed up at me, her smile white and innocent. 'Remember how we talked about me taking better care of myself?'

I nodded.

'Well, today I went to the doctor and then went to the salon and splurged on getting my hair done.'

'Good girl.' I pressed a kiss to her mouth. 'Everything okay... with the doctor?'

'Yeah. I, um, got put on birth control.'

This time I couldn't help the smile tugging on my mouth. My wide grin told her this knowledge made me very happy. Knowing I could be inside her without any barrier produced a caveman-like response in me. I'd always used condoms. Always. But McKenna was trusting me, giving herself to me fully. The thought was intoxicating.

'That's...' I choked on the words and this time McKenna was the one laughing at me.

'You like that, don't you?' she teased. 'Good, because I got a shot in my butt today for you.'

Bringing both hands down to her backside, I rubbed her ass cheeks gently. 'My poor girl.' Nuzzling into her neck, I gave her a few slow, damp kisses as I moved closer to her mouth. 'I'll take good care of you tonight,' I murmured against her skin. It occurred to me she didn't have any of her stuff here—nothing to sleep in, no toothbrush. It made me realize I needed to take better care of my girl, make sure she felt comfortable here.

She dropped her head to the side, giving me better access to her neck, her fingers still tracing little circles on my back, underneath my shirt. 'You said we needed to celebrate. What did you have in mind?'

My lips curled in a smile as I planted a kiss on the spot just beneath her ear. 'You sure you can handle it?'

She nodded eagerly.

My fingers found the hem of her shirt and I began to lift it over her head, my body all too ready to show her all the ways she was mine.

'Wait.' Her hands stopped me. 'You said there was more we needed to discuss.'

I faltered, swallowing a lump in my throat. 'Yeah. Ah, I wanted to tell you, you wanting to help Luke…if it's what you want, that's cool with me.'

'Yeah?' she asked.

'Yeah,' I confirmed. 'You and him work out the details. I trust you.'

'You're being so good tonight.' She patted my chest. 'Very cooperative.'

God, it had been too long since we'd had a night like this, one where we could be playful and just enjoy each other. There had been too much shit swirling over both of us lately, and though I knew I should say more, something in me couldn't. We deserved tonight. We deserved to just enjoy each other.

'Now, where were we?' I pulled her close so our bodies were pressed tightly together and took her mouth in a hungry kiss, gripping the back of her neck to hold her close to me. McKenna moaned into my kiss, angling her mouth to mine. She was so responsive, so needy, and the dominant lurking inside me fucking loved it.

My cell phone vibrated in my pocket and McKenna let out a soft whimper as the buzzing device pressed against the front of her jeans.

I chuckled at her response. She liked that. Good to know. 'One second, baby.' I released her and tugged the phone from my pocket. I was going to toss it on my dresser, get rid of the interruption, but Jaxon's name flashed on the screen.

Shit. Nice timing, asshole. 'You better be dead or dying,' I bit out as I answered the call.

McKenna swatted at me again. 'Be nice,' she mouthed.

'Close,' Jaxon croaked. 'I'm at Regency Hospital. In the ER. Can you come get me?'

'What the fuck? What happened?'

'I got jumped. I'll explain when you get here.'

Motherfucker. 'On my way.'

'What's wrong? What happened?' McKenna's worried gaze met mine.

'Jaxon's in trouble again. Can you stay here with the boys?'

Her hand flew to her mouth and she nodded.

Adjusting my raging boner, I fled down the stairs.

When Jaxon and I arrived home, I didn't care that he could hardly walk or see out of eyes nearly swollen shut—I made him march up the stairs to his room. I didn't want him sleeping on the couch and the sorry sight of him to be the first thing Tucker saw when he woke up in the morning.

'Get to bed. We'll talk about this in the morning.'

Jaxon huffed. 'If I don't get them their money, there will be nothing to talk about. I'm telling you, man, this crew is ruthless.'

I fisted my hands at my sides, fighting the urge to punch the wall. 'We'll figure it out.' I had no idea how, but of course the responsibility would fall on me.

Apparently we'd made enough of a racket that we'd woken McKenna. She peeked inside the room, gazing in with wide eyes. 'Oh God.' Her hand flew to her mouth. 'Jax…' She crossed the room and pressed one hand to his cheek. He winced at the contact and she withdrew. 'What happened?' A lone tear rolled down her face and I took a deep breath, fighting to calm myself down.

'He was beaten within an inch of his life over a gambling debt. They dropped him off at the emergency room and promised this time was just a warning if he doesn't pay back what he owes,' I answered for him.

McKenna's gaze left mine and searched Jaxon's. He looked guilty. I knew he felt as terrible as he looked, which was the only thing helping me contain my rage.

41

'Jax…why?' she asked.

'I was trying to help.'

I cursed under my breath and pressed my fingers against my temples.

Jaxon hobbled closer, scowling as he met my gaze. He looked every bit as pissed off as I felt. 'I'm not a kid, Knox. I know you're struggling with the money for Luke's college, and that shouldn't be what ruins this for him. Or for you and McKenna. You're a dick when you get stressed out and you make stupid fucking decisions. You're happy, like actually happy for the first time in a long time, and Luke…Luke deserves to go to college. I was doing my part. You're not the only one who can take care of this family.'

'This was your way of taking care of things? Fuck. Next time, get a job. You know, something actually legal that's not going to end up costing me money to bail your ass out.'

'Don't be mad at Jax,' McKenna chimed in. 'He was trying to help. Even if it wasn't in the right way, his intentions were in the right place.'

'He's fucking eighteen years old, McKenna. He's an adult. He knows better.'

Jaxon collapsed onto his unmade bed, lying back and releasing a heavy sigh. 'If I don't pay them back…'

'I know.' I clenched my jaw. I knew the group of guys he'd bet and lost against. A local street gang of thugs. Even if I didn't like the idea of caving to their demands, I knew he was right. They wouldn't stop until they had fucked us over, and this beating was the tip of the iceberg in terms of what they were capable of. I couldn't have them going after Luke or Tuck. We needed to take care of this.

'How much do you owe?' McKenna asked, her voice whisper soft.

'Twenty-five thousand,' Jaxon said, not meeting my eyes.

'Fuck, no, McKenna. This isn't on you to fix.' This was not what I envisioned when I told her she could help Luke.

Luke entered the room and closed the door behind him. 'You guys need to lower your voices unless we want to turn this into a family meeting.' He grimaced when he saw Jaxon. 'Shit, bro.'

Christ, the last thing we needed was Tucker getting up. Although if I was being honest, I knew Jaxon's injuries would look worse tomorrow. His eyes were already nearly swollen shut and his lip was busted apart and huge. By morning the bruises would begin to turn purple. He clutched his ribs and toed off his shoes. McKenna knelt beside his bed to help him.

'Everyone out. Jaxon needs his sleep.' Luke and I started for the door when McKenna's hand flew up, stopping us.

'Wait.' She swallowed and straightened her shoulders. 'I have the money. I was going to give it to Luke for college…'

Luke's gaze flew to hers and a smile blossomed on his mouth.

'But…' she continued. 'It sounds like at the moment, making sure Jax doesn't end up dead is more important.'

Luke's smile fell and he shot a murderous look at Jaxon. Jax closed his eyes, obviously unable to watch the disappointment looming in Luke's expression.

'We don't have health insurance, so this little adventure at the hospital tonight is going to cost us, too,' Luke added.

Shit, he was right. As much as I hated the idea of McKenna bailing us out, I realized we had little choice. I might have been okay with her helping Luke out, giving him money toward his education, but I hated the idea of her throwing away her money toward Jaxon's criminal enterprises. I would pay her back every penny. And I would make sure Luke still got to go to college too. Somehow.

'We'll figure this out tomorrow.'

My tone was final and McKenna nodded. I doubted sleep would come tonight, as wound up as I was, but we headed up the stairs and climbed into bed, deafening silence hanging all around us.

Chapter Six

McKenna

In the morning, the harsh reality of the situation with Jaxon pushed itself into the forefront of my brain. I rolled over and tugged the blankets up higher, snuggling into Knox's side, trying to pretend for a few minutes more that all this wasn't happening. A quick peek at Knox told me he'd been awake for hours. He was lying still but staring straight up at the ceiling, looking lost in thought.

I sat up in bed, looking down at his dark, troubled expression. We needed to do something, not just cave to this gang's demands. 'Knox?'

He glanced over at me, the crease between his brows softening just slightly when he met my eyes.

I took his hand, giving it a squeeze and letting him know we were in this together. I was here and I would help in any way I could. 'We should call the police. They jumped Jaxon. And we can't just turn over this much money.' Now that it was morning, I was thinking more rationally about the situation.

Silence hung heavily in the room around us. 'No police, angel,' he said. 'These guys will just retaliate if we get the police involved. Last year something similar happened—a guy who owed them payment for gambling debts talked to the police when they got too rough with him, and the next day they put a bullet in his head.'

Knox looked back up at the ceiling, his mouth pulling into a tight line. 'I won't put any of us at risk. Money isn't worth any of our lives. And I'll pay you back every cent, I promise.'

I started to wave him off; this wasn't about money. I didn't care about Knox paying me back, but the grim expression etched across his face told me now was not the time to argue. I gave an imperceptible nod. 'Okay,' I whispered. We'd do things his way. This was his family, and I knew he'd protect them the best way he knew how. All I could do was be there for them.

I dressed in yesterday's clothes and kissed Knox good-bye, and after heading home to shower and change, I went to the bank. It turned out getting twenty-five thousand dollars in cash was a lot more difficult than I expected. After meeting with a teller, an assistant manager, and then the bank branch manager, I headed off to work. They would have my money by the end of the day. It would take them several hours to get it all together.

I sent Knox a text. I didn't know if something would happen to Jaxon in the meantime, but I figured the men who had threatened him would give him some time to get the cash together.

Me: *I'm coming over tonight with the money.*

Knox: *I don't like this.*

Me: *Me neither. But we have to do it.*

He didn't respond and unease churned inside me all day long. I hated thinking that he'd try to take matters into his own hands today, try to persuade the guys who'd done this to Jaxon. I couldn't have something happening to Knox, too. Brian was barely healed and now Jaxon was lying in bed, broken and beaten up. We just had to bite the bullet and pay the gang off. This had to work.

Thankful I still had my rental car, when I left work I drove straight to the bank again. The bank manager looked at me as if I were crazy when he handed me the backpack full of stacked bills. He asked again and again if I was okay. I think he thought

45

I was being bribed or threatened into withdrawing this money. Well, I was, sort of. Someone I cared about would be badly hurt if I didn't fix this.

As I headed back to Knox's, Brian called to let me know he would be back in the morning, but I could barely concentrate on what he was saying.

When I arrived at Knox's place, he looked ready to murder someone. He was pacing the floor in the living room and his brows were drawn together, his eyes hard and fierce. I'd never seen him so worked up.

I held up the backpack. 'I brought it.'

He nodded and crossed the room toward me, then immediately gathered me up in his arms and pressed a firm kiss to my forehead.

I hated to admit it, but he was scaring me. My knees trembled and my stomach felt queasy. I had no way of knowing if this was all going to turn out okay and I couldn't lose another person I loved. I couldn't. The desperate need to never let him go, to stay by his side tonight, clawed at me. 'I'm coming with you.'

He shook his head. 'Not happening.'

'Knox—'

His mouth closed over mine and the rough edge to his kiss killed my protest. He was a desperate man, doing what needed to be done to protect his family. But it was obvious there'd be no negotiating this. I realized he had no choice taking my help with the money, but it was obvious that was where my involvement ended. I didn't want to argue and push him when it seemed like he was already at the edge of his control. I knew what happened when he lost control; I wouldn't push him there willingly. If staying behind at the house was the way I could protect him and preserve his sense of calm, I would do it.

'I want to keep you safe. Stay here with Luke and Tucker.'

I released a heavy exhale and nodded. 'Okay.'

'Lock the doors and don't answer if someone comes knocking.'

I nodded again, my stomach cramping with nerves. *Jeez.*

'If anything happens to us, call the police.'

Oh God. I couldn't handle something happening to Knox. Tears filled my eyes.

'Hey, shhh, it's okay,' he whispered, brushing his knuckles along my cheek. 'We'll be all right. Stay strong.'

He was right; I needed to pull myself together. I didn't want to alert Tucker that anything was wrong. I blinked the tears away and fixed a neutral expression on my face. I just had to have faith.

Jaxon looked even worse today. I had no idea what story they gave Tucker, but Jaxon looked every bit like he'd been jumped and brutally beaten. His eyes were swollen and puffy, heavy blackish-purple circles lining each one, and he was limping slightly, holding a hand to his side. His ribs were either bruised or broken, and part of me didn't even want to ask.

I wanted to rush to him and take him in my arms, but I merely met his eyes with a sympathetic stare and he gave me a tight nod. Even though this was pretty much the world's crappiest situation, it brought me closer into this family, and I had to say I loved that.

Watching Knox converse in hushed tones with Jaxon and Luke, I was struck with a pang of shock. Before I met Knox, I was so naive. I never knew even half of the things that went on in this world. I had been living in my own bubble of misery, volunteering and just existing. Still, I wouldn't trade this for anything. Even though times were tough, I had a family again. A big, messy family, complete with love, heartache, and worry. My emotions were right at the surface today and everything felt so raw and new. I was out of practice with this whole family thing, and felt vulnerable and exposed.

Luke and I watched them prepare to leave, exchanging equally worried expressions between us. Luke, seeming to realize he was now the oldest brother in charge, came to stand beside me and placed a comforting arm around my shoulders, giving me a squeeze. 'It'll be okay, McKenna. Knox will handle this.' His voice sounded calm and certain, but he had no way of knowing the outcome, any more than I did.

I just nodded. I trusted Knox; I just didn't trust this shady neighborhood street gang. Once they'd gotten this money from us, would they really leave us alone?

Shrugging on the backpack, Knox crossed the room and kissed me full on the mouth. He rarely did that in front of his brothers, but I met his kiss with my own fierce edge, letting my tongue briefly rub against his. His hands cupping my face trembled ever so slightly. 'I love you,' he whispered.

I nodded. 'Love you, too.' My eyes screamed at him to stay safe and come home to me in one piece.

He nodded in silent acknowledgement of my request. 'We'll be fine.'

My stomach dropped to my toes and for the first time, I could relate to Knox's fears and hesitations when it came to love. If I didn't love them all so much, this process wouldn't be nearly as scary. I gripped Luke tighter and said a silent prayer that Knox knew what he was doing.

Several hours later and everyone was in bed, but I was way too amped up to sleep. I paced Knox's bedroom, my heart heavy with worry. *Where were they? What was taking so long?*

I checked my phone for the hundredth time and fell back onto his bed. I curled into the pillow that held Knox's unique scent, inhaling deeply. Warm leather and male musk, a delicious combination.

A short time later, I awoke to the sound of someone climbing the stairs.

Knox was back.

I sat up in bed, rubbing the sleep from my tired eyes. *Oh, thank God. He was okay.*

Knox stood in the doorway, smiling at me like everything was right with the world, and the tense knot that had taken up residence in my stomach uncurled in an instant. His brilliant smile melted my heart and the hardened shield I'd erected in his absence.

He tossed the backpack onto the bed and it landed with a dull thud. It was still full. I lifted it to my lap and unzipped it. The cash was still stacked inside.

'What happened…how did you?'

Dread sank low in the pit of my stomach. They hadn't succeeded tonight. Which meant the gang was probably coming for us. My mind was already running through scenarios of us five holed up in my apartment. I needed to buy groceries, milk, get more towels…

'McKenna.' Knox's warm hands cupped my cheeks. 'Look at me.'

My gaze drifted back to him and I took a deep breath. *Just breathe.*

'You didn't think I was just going to watch them walk away with Luke's college fund, did you?'

That was exactly what I'd assumed. That was the plan, wasn't it? I wouldn't have offered the money if I hadn't thought it was the only way. 'I don't understand.'

I listened with bated breath while Knox filled me in on how he'd contacted his lawyer and provided the tip that this exchange was going down tonight. His lawyer agreed to inform the police; that way the call could never be traced back to Knox. Several members of the gang were wanted on various charges, and once the cops had the time and meeting place of tonight's exchange, they showed up and apprehended the bad guys. Knox and Jaxon took off running—well, hobbling in Jaxon's case—and hid out until the police had made their arrests and taken the gang members away to keep up the ruse Jaxon and Knox weren't responsible for involving the police. Once the scene was clear, the money was returned to Knox.

I shook my head in disbelief. I couldn't believe he'd put himself in danger, orchestrating that entire thing without me knowing. I felt sick thinking about what could have gone wrong. It was probably better that he hadn't told me about his alternative plan; my head would have been spinning with *what ifs*. Saving this money was not worth the risk.

'Knox, you guys could have…' *Been killed.* I couldn't even bring myself to speak the words. Hot tears leaked from the corners of my eyes. Why would he take such a risk? I couldn't lose him.

He took my hands and held them. 'That is your money to do what you want with. Your parents worked hard to earn that, saved for years to make sure you would be okay. Even if I don't love the idea of you giving it to Luke, I get it. It's who you are. It's one of the reasons I love you. That money is yours to do what you want with. There was no way I was just handing it over.'

'But how did you know this would all work out? That you could trust this lawyer and the police to—'

'Shhh. It's over now.' He kissed me softly on the mouth.

My whirling thoughts and racing heart felt anything but comforted. 'Are you sure it's not going to come back to you? They could find out you set this up. How do you know this lawyer, anyway?' Questions tumbled from my lips as my brain fought to catch up.

His gaze slid away from mine. 'It's been a long night. We'll talk about that later.' Opening his arms, he urged me closer. 'Come here.'

I sensed there was something he wasn't telling me, and a flicker of curiosity bloomed inside me, but I let it go and curled against his side, savoring the feel of his firm body against mine. Knowing how close I could have come to losing him tonight quieted me and I clung to him, desperate for skin-to-skin contact.

Chapter Seven

Knox

I tugged McKenna closer, pushing my hand under the T-shirt she wore to bed, unable to resist running my hand along the soft curve of her ass. Tonight had been stressful—leading Jaxon into a situation like that and involving the police, which totally went against my gut and had put me on edge. But there was no way I was letting McKenna take the hit for Jaxon's mistake. That money belonged to her. I wasn't about to let it fall into the hands of a street gang. She deserved to be in control of her parent's inheritance, and even if she wanted to use it to fund Luke's education, it was hers to do with what she wanted.

'What are you doing?' She giggled as my hand squeezed her ass cheek.

'Just exploring,' I growled near her ear. I hoped she wasn't too tired, because I needed to feel her around me. Tonight more than ever.

'How can you be thinking about sex right now?' she teased, wiggling her ass farther away from me. 'You could have been killed tonight.'

'But I wasn't.' I tugged her close again. No way was I letting her escape that easy. 'And now I want to celebrate by getting my cock wet in your sweet honey.' It was crude, but I wasn't in the mood to sugarcoat my mood with pretty words. I hitched her bare leg up over my hip so she could feel that I was already semi-hard for her.

51

'You and your insatiable boners.' She rolled her eyes for dramatic effect. Her playful mood was exactly what I needed to relax. And studying me in the dim light, McKenna seemed to understand that. 'The things I do for my sex-addicted boyfriend.' She sighed.

Boyfriend. I liked that word coming from her lips. 'I'm addicted to your tight, hot pussy. And I'm not going to apologize for that.'

'So, what are you going to do about it?' she challenged, a lively spark in her eyes.

I pulled her over the top of me so she was straddling my lap. I loved the weight of her against me, the sight of her sitting on top of me. Tugging her panties to the side, I touched my fingertips to her pussy lips, finding them glistening with her moisture, and my cock swelled even more. 'I want to feel your heat squeezing my cock.'

McKenna let out a helpless whimper.

I continued rubbing her, spreading her apart so I could stroke her clit in a little circular pattern that made her hips rock slightly against mine, and nestled my cock nice and tight between her ass cheeks.

'Careful, angel. I'm tempted to bury myself inside you, and if that happens I don't know if I can hold back tonight.'

She breathed my name, her head dropping back as she pushed her hips closer, greedy for more friction against her pleasure spot. A firm grip and a twist of the fabric and I tore the panties from her body, tossing them aside. 'Oops,' I deadpanned.

She watched me with wide eyes, her pulse frantically thrumming at the base of her throat. She liked this side of me. *Good girl.*

Lifting her weight with one hand, I pushed my cotton boxers down my thighs with the other, freeing my cock to rest between us. Rocking her hips against me, her wet pussy slid along my shaft, coating me in her juices. A growl rose from my throat. I cursed under my breath, my hands clutching into fists at my sides.

Restraint was not my strong point, and she was making me crazy with desire. I was about three seconds away from pounding into her, brutally taking everything she was offering.

'You better stop me now, angel, unless you want me to fuck you bare.' I knew her birth control hadn't kicked in yet, but shit, in that moment, I was willing to risk it. I needed her. Just her, with no barrier between us. She made me want things I never thought I'd want. She made me crazy with the desire to not only fuck her, but to consume her from the inside out.

'Give it to me,' she breathed. Her confidence and husky tone caused a drop of fluid to leak from my tip.

Positioning the head of my cock at her entrance, I pushed forward slowly but steadily, easing past the tightness of her inner muscles and not stopping until I was completely buried deep inside her body. McKenna let out a low murmur of discomfort. I knew I was testing her, pushing her limits, but I also knew she liked it. And I loved the feel of her stretching around me.

'Ride me, angel,' I encouraged, placing one hand against her side, my thumb lightly stroking her hip bone.

She rotated her hips, drawing me even deeper and savoring the feel of me buried so completely, before lifting and lowering herself back down in tiny increments as she adjusted to my size.

Watching her hips move against mine, seeing her eyes slip closed as an expression of ecstasy overtook her features was too much. *Fuck*. She was my everything.

I gripped her hips, lifting her up and down while I planted my feet against the mattress and used the leverage to thrust into her. Unable to hold back, I pounded into her tight little pussy over and over again, loving the way her chest bounced as I plunged into her.

All too soon, McKenna was exploding around me, murmuring my name and gripping her breasts to rub her nipples as she started to come.

The sight of her, coupled with the intense way her body gripped at mine, wrenched the last of my self-control away. Tingles at the base of my spine drew my balls tight against my body as my own release began. Hot jets of semen pumped into her. McKenna clung to me helplessly and I lifted up on my elbows to kiss her. Her walls continued pulsing around me for several seconds as our breathing slowed and our kiss turned deeper, slower.

One thing was certain: I did not deserve an angel like McKenna. The only explanation for her presence in my life was that my mom had sent her from heaven to look after us all. It was the only thing that made sense. I'd known she was my angel right from the very beginning.

I wanted to make love to her over and over again, taking my time like it might be my last time touching her. The last time I had the privilege of holding her naked body against mine. Because when she found out about my connection to the lawyer, I was all too aware that all of this could end.

Chapter Eight

McKenna

Amanda and her baby girl, AnnMarie—named for both of her grandmas—were being released from the hospital today. And since I felt so guilty that I hadn't even visited once, I'd offered to pick her up and give them a ride home. Just as I was stepping into my shoes and shrugging on my coat, Brian opened the door to our apartment.

'I wasn't expecting you until later,' I said with surprise. 'Did you drive yourself?'

He lifted his arms out to his sides. 'Good as new. Not even a limp. I can operate a car and everything.'

Much-needed laughter bubbled its way up my throat. The last few days had been too tense, and it was good to see his smiling face.

He gathered me in his arms for a hug. 'Damn, it's good to be home,' he said.

'It's good to see you on your feet.'

'Where are you off to?' he asked, taking in my appearance.

'I was actually going to pick up a friend and her brand new baby from the hospital, then drive them home.'

'You still have that rental car?' he asked.

I nodded sheepishly. 'I was supposed to return it days ago. But it turns out I like having my own wheels.'

Brian chuckled. 'How about this. I'll follow you to the rental lot so you can return it, and then I'll give you a lift to the hospital so we can get your friend.'

I nodded. 'If you don't mind, that would be really helpful.'

'Are you kidding? I've been in a bed for almost a month. The last thing I want to do is sit inside alone and watch more TV.'

He dropped his bags in his bedroom, used the restroom, and then we were on the road within minutes. As promised, Brian followed me to the rental lot and waited while I returned the rental car and paid the bill, then we were en route to the hospital.

'So…you and Knox…' he started.

When I was in Indiana for all those weeks, Brian knew my relationship with Knox was on the rocks. Now he was fishing for information, but I couldn't blame him. He had to be curious, and I'd been pretty closed off about my relationship.

'We're back together. I love him, Bri. I love being with him and his brothers. And I think my parents would have wanted me to be happy.'

He nodded silently, looking out at the road. 'Yeah, they would have,' he said after several minutes of silence. 'They would be really proud of you, you know.'

It was the first time I'd heard him acknowledge that, and irrational tears filled my eyes.

'Guess it's time I let you go,' he said softly. 'Shit, I've had a crush on you since the first grade. You can't say I didn't try.'

I chuckled lightly. 'You put in a valiant effort.'

He reached over and took my hand. 'Knox is lucky to have you.'

'Thanks, Bri.'

His injury and time recouping seemed to bring him a new sense of peace and clarity. It had given him a lot of time to think. And my leaving him while he was still recovering to return to Knox must have sent a stronger message than I realized. I'd chosen Knox over him in every way possible.

When we arrived at the hospital, we checked in at the security desk and were directed to the third-floor maternity wing. I thought Brian might just wait for us in the waiting room, but he insisted on helping, saying there would probably be bags to carry.

I decided I liked his new helpfulness and sense of peace about our friends-only status. We paused outside Amanda's room and I gave a knock on the door.

'Come in!' she called, her voice sounding clear and happy.

I poked my head in and made sure she was dressed. She was wearing stretch pants and a cute top, and had a big smile across her face.

'I have my friend Brian with me…that okay?' I asked.

She nodded. 'Of course. Thanks for coming.' She waved us in.

We entered the room and I gave Amanda a big hug before peeking inside the bassinet holding the tiny baby.

'Aw…' I gushed as a rush of emotions hit me at once. Amanda was a mom. And AnnMarie was so tiny and pink. She was absolutely precious. A miracle baby in more ways than one.

While I held the baby and cuddled her in the nearby rocking chair, I was vaguely aware of Amanda and Brian getting to know each other. *Oops.* Apparently I'd forgotten my manners along with making formal introductions as soon as I'd seen the baby. But Brian was standing with his hands in his pockets and a big grin on his face, and Amanda was laughing at something he'd said, so I focused on the sweet little thing in my arms again. She was so light, I could hold her forever. Her little pink face turned up to mine, and she lazily peeked open one eye and yawned. I couldn't help but giggle.

'So she's all good, despite being born early?' I asked.

Amanda nodded, pulling her attention away from Brian. 'Yeah, she's good to go. She had a hard time regulating her body temperature, which is why we had to stay a couple extra days, but she's completely healthy. She's almost five pounds already, and eats like a horse.'

The pride in Amanda's smile touched something inside me. It seemed we were all growing.

'So I hear we're here to spring you out of here,' Brian said, looking at Amanda again.

'Yes, I'm more than ready to leave. It's impossible to get a decent night's sleep with nurses coming in every couple of hours and turning on the lights, poking this, prodding that.'

I handed her daughter back to her. 'I hate to tell you this, but I think your nights of sleeping are over.'

'Yeah, I know.' She smiled down at the baby in her arms. 'But she's worth it.'

'May I?' Brian asked, stopping in front of Amanda and looking down at the baby.

'Oh, sure,' she said and passed him the infant.

Watching Brian hold the baby only made her look tinier. He cooed something unintelligible down at her while Amanda and I swooned. What was it about a man and a baby?

While Amanda bundled AnnMarie up in the car seat, Brian and I gathered up her bags. 'Do you have everything you need at home?' I asked. I knew the birth had been a surprise, and aside from our thrift-store shopping a while back, I didn't know if she was prepared to take the baby home.

'I have a bassinet for her to sleep in, diapers, wipes, and some clothes. I'm breastfeeding because it's, well, it's free and I can't afford baby formula. Besides, it's not as bad as I thought it'd be. So yeah, I think we have everything we need.'

I nodded. 'Okay.' It sounded like she had the essentials covered. I realized babies really didn't need much. Despite all the plastic gear and baby products on the market, Amanda was embracing the simple side of things.

Brian's brows scrunched together. 'If you need anything else, you let us know. Any friend of McKenna's is a friend of mine.'

Amanda smiled up at him. 'I will.'

His offer was sweet. I wondered if his demeanor would change if I told him how I knew Amanda, and that she was an addict in recovery I'd met in group. Or maybe his harsh criticism was only reserved for Knox. Either way, I let it go. Today was a happy day, and it felt like everyone was heading in the right direction.

Chapter Nine

McKenna

With the drama of the last few days behind us, I wanted to make the most of my time with Knox. We needed to be alone, to just reconnect. I loved that he'd planned a date for us, and deciding that I quite liked having a boyfriend, I wanted to return the favor. I wanted to go somewhere we could both relax and enjoy the day together. And I'd told Belinda that despite returning to Chicago after my extended leave of absence, she should give my Saturday morning sex-addict group to my replacement permanently.

Which meant both Knox and I were free on Saturdays now. My new schedule felt positively decadent. Having time to actually pursue a relationship was something new for me. The old me would have felt guilty. The new me was going to enjoy every minute of it.

When Knox picked me up later that afternoon, I slid into the warmth of his Jeep, inhaling his masculine scent and instantly feeling happy and secure.

'Are you okay with me being in charge today?' I smiled at him.

His gaze jerked over to mine and an unexpected jab of lust shot straight between my thighs at the wicked grin on his lips. 'I think I can handle that. Where to, angel?'

'Downtown,' I answered. 'Park somewhere near Lakeshore Drive.'

He was dressed in a warm-looking thermal tee and a black fleece, and since it wasn't totally freezing out today, my plan should work.

Once he'd parallel parked on a side street just off Lakeshore Drive, I laced his fingers with mine and led him down to the walking path bordering the lake. It was the middle of January, which meant we were completely alone on the beach. Just me, Knox, and the endless blue water stretched out before us, gently lapping at the sandy shoreline.

We huddled into our coats and almost by instinct, our joined hands squeezed tighter. It was just us. No kids. No Brian or Amanda. No drama. I breathed in a deep, refreshing lungful of fresh air and sighed happily.

We walked side by side in silence for a few moments, and though it looked like there was something heavy on his mind, when I questioned Knox, the tension in his features fell away and he dropped a kiss to my mouth.

'Everything's perfect, angel,' he assured me.

Perhaps it was still lingering worry over Jaxon. Either way, I dismissed it. Knox was by my side and that was all that mattered. I was learning to let the past go, to stay in the moment and enjoy.

I nestled closer into his side, inhaling his intoxicating scent.

'Are you cold?' he asked, leaning down to press a kiss against my temple.

Not with his big body to shield me from the wind. 'Not really, no.'

'So, are we gonna talk about things now that you're back?' he asked.

'Like?' I prompted.

'Like your many volunteering jobs, where you live, and when you're going to buy a car and stop taking the bus.' He raised an eyebrow at me.

I remembered feeling protected and cared for right from the first time I'd gone to Knox's house—he was so against me taking the bus across town on my own. He'd insisted on personally escorting me home. He'd wormed his way into my heart right from the beginning, even if I didn't see it at the time. All the signs were there. He was a good man. Or maybe I was the exception, since I was pretty sure he hadn't always treated women with such care and respect.

I glanced over at him to address his questions. 'As for volunteering, I'm no longer leading the Saturday morning group.' I was guessing he'd figured as much since I hadn't in a couple of months now. 'A car is on my to-do list. Brian said he'd help me look.'

'I'll take you, McKenna.' His look said not to argue.

Okay then. Knox will help me get a car.

I nodded and continued. 'And what about where I live?' I paused, waiting for him to give me some clue about what he'd meant. My apartment with Brian was in a safe part of town. I didn't see what issue he could possibly take up there.

He stopped walking and turned to face me. The sunlight glinting in his beautiful eyes showed off shades of moss green and warm brown. He released my hand, only to bring both of his palms up to cup my face. 'When you were away, I realized something about myself. I love you, McKenna, and I don't want to be without you. I want you to move in with me.'

The air felt trapped in my chest as I processed his words. He wanted me. He loved me. His offer was much more significant than he could have known. He was giving me my family back. The piece of me that had been missing for all these years. A warm home filled with love and activity. Tears welled in my eyes.

'Knox…' I sobbed, inhaling ragged breaths.

'Shhh. Don't answer now. I know it's a lot to process, something you probably want to think about. But I promise you one thing—I'm never going back to the man I was before. You've changed me. You came into my life and completely fucking gutted me. I thought I couldn't love again, but you were right all along. Love was the exact thing I was missing and searching for in all those women.'

I flinched slightly at his words. Being reminded of his past wasn't easy, but his thumb brushed across my bottom lip, deliciously distracting me.

'I was looking for you the entire time. And it took a downward spiral for me to find you. My angel,' he whispered.

I wanted to tell him yes, of course I would move in, but my lips were busy attacking his. I kissed him with a brutal force that he matched with swipe after swipe of his tongue against mine. He hauled me closer, one hand still cupping my face, and the other pressed against my butt to align our bodies together. Suddenly being in public seemed like a terrible idea.

'Knox…' I breathed against his damp lips.

'Yeah?' His voice was a rough growl that sent delicious vibrations spiraling through me.

'Let's go somewhere.'

'My house,' he answered.

Yes. Please. Anywhere but here. Preferably somewhere with a bed. 'Wait.' I pulled back. 'Won't your brothers be there?'

His hazy eyes found mine. 'They know we fuck, McKenna.' He pressed his erection against my belly and rubbed it against me.

A whimper fell from my parted lips and I couldn't argue. I nodded quickly and he led me back to his Jeep. I almost laughed as I tried to keep up with Knox's pace. His long legs ate up the sidewalk and I pranced alongside him. We'd made it fifteen minutes into our date before we cracked and needed to be alone. But there was no denying my entire body was humming with need. He'd created this side of me. And I was all too happy to go along with it.

We climbed inside the Jeep and Knox wasted no time cranking the ignition and pulling out into traffic. A silent glance in his direction caused a knot to form in my stomach. He was still rock hard in his jeans, the rigid weight of his erection clearly visible through the denim. Desire pulsed through me, hot and uncontained.

'Knox…' I murmured.

His hand curled around the back of my neck, guiding my mouth to his while he maintained eye contact with the road. 'Not long, baby,' he assured me, his lips brushing against mine.

I pressed my thighs together, squirming in the seat as his warm tongue licked against my bottom lip. I knew what delicious, naughty things his tongue could do to other parts of my body. A flash of moisture dampened my panties.

I'd survived so long without physical affection and sex, maybe now I was making up for lost time. Either that or Knox alone had unleashed something in me that refused to be contained. Especially now that I knew how good he could make me feel.

When Knox broke the kiss, I found myself unable to resist. I reached across the center console and curled my hand around the hard ridge in his pants, eliciting a soft groan from him.

I rubbed his firm length up and down, loving how big and masculine he felt in my hand. I wanted to make him feel good and lose all control like he did to me. I wanted to see him come apart.

'Shit,' he cursed, his hands gripping the wheel until his knuckles turned white.

I wanted to unbutton his pants, tug down his zipper and free his cock, feel its warm weight against my skin, in my mouth, but I settled for lightly stroking him over his pants.

The raspy breath shuddering in his chest was the only encouragement I needed. Using my fingernails, I lightly raked across him, squeezing and caressing him. I might have said this was for him—meant to turn him on and drive him wild—but it was just as much for me. Touching him, knowing I was bringing him pleasure, made me feel sexy and powerful. Not to mention how it drenched my panties with my own arousal.

Thankfully, we soon pulled to a stop in the driveway behind his house and Knox turned to face me.

'You're going to regret teasing me, angel.'

The husky tone of his voice and ragged breathing, coupled with the sight of his raging erection, made my stomach flip. I was playing a dangerous game, but there was no way I was stopping now.

He sucked in a few deep breaths, and adjusted the monstrosity in his pants before climbing from the Jeep.

Unlocking the back door, he led me inside. All was peaceful in the house. Tucker and Luke were in the living room, Tuck watching cartoons and Luke busy typing away on the laptop.

Knox and I crept up the stairs without so much as a hello. I felt a little villainous, sneaking off to do naughty things with him, but it was a feeling I liked. I was embracing the bad-girl side of myself that only Knox brought out.

Once we were safely tucked inside his bedroom, with the door locked and closed behind us, Knox's hungry gaze caught mine and I felt trapped. I was his. Completely at his mercy. He stalked toward me like he was the hunter and I was the hunted.

Not bothering to cross the room to the bed, he pinned me against the wall, his large frame swallowing mine as he pressed his body close. He rubbed his large erection against my belly.

'You wanted to tease me, make me want you, but not let me come… That wasn't nice, angel.'

I let out a helpless whimper. I hadn't meant to be mean.

His mouth caught mine, taking my bottom lip between his teeth and tugging it gently. 'Naughty girls like you need to be taught a lesson.'

'Are you going to punish me?' I whispered, my lips brushing his.

'I'm going to make sure you never forget who's in charge.' He lifted my shirt from over my head and tossed it behind him, then he found the clasp on my bra and removed that next. The cool air nipped at me, sending goose bumps across my belly and puckering my nipples. His gaze slipped lower and landed on my breasts. 'So pretty,' he said, his thumbs lightly stroking the sensitive pink flesh. A gasp stuck in my throat. His hands were warm and I savored the rough feel of his fingertips against me.

'Knox,' I breathed.

'Shhh. You forgot already, angel, I'm setting the pace today.'

A frustrated whimper escaped my lips and I leaned forward to kiss him. If I could drive him wild, maybe I could get him to move things along faster. I reached for his belt buckle and his mouth moved against mine in a low, throaty chuckle.

'No way, sweetheart. You're not playing with my cock again until I'm ready for you to. Hands clasped behind you.'

Fighting the urge to roll my eyes, I laced my fingers behind me, which only caused my breasts to stick out more.

Knox's wet mouth closed over one nipple, and with his eyes on mine to watch my reaction, he sucked and licked my nipple until it was distended into a firm peak. Then he flicked his tongue back and forth across the other while I watched in agonized pleasure.

His fingers worked at the button of my jeans, then he slowly lowered the zipper and tugged them open to push them down my hips. My panties went next as Knox roughly shoved them down my legs until I could step out of them. I stood before him completely undressed as the chill of the room nipped at me and desire burned hotly inside. The effect was dizzying.

Keeping my fingers laced behind me, I raised up on my toes, needing to be closer to him in any way I could. I nuzzled against his neck, stroking my nose against his rough skin and inhaling his scent. 'Can I kiss you?' I murmured.

'Of course.'

I captured his mouth in a hot, hungry kiss, my tongue lightly stroking his while his hands curled around my hips, squeezing as though he was just barely holding back from taking me right here, right now. To which I'd have no objections.

Using his grip around my hips, Knox lifted me and I wrapped my legs around his waist, enjoying the sensation of the hard ridge in his denim pressing into my bottom as he carried me over to his bed. *Finally.*

He tossed me down onto the mattress and looked down at me for just a second before pulling his shirt off over his head. I loved studying the dips and planes in his abdominals and pecs. I could stare at this man all day; he was a work of art. So masculine and strong, both inside and out. His hands caught his belt and I watched as if in a trance as he slowly undid the buckle and pulled his cock free. He was thick and swollen with need, a large vein running the length of him.

Unable to resist, I rose on my hands and knees and brought my mouth to him, running my tongue along that pulsing vein, teasing, licking, and tasting his smooth length. A low murmur escaped his throat and my core clenched with need. I gripped his shaft, rubbing both hands up and down as my mouth continued to hover over him, licking and sucking all along his steely cock.

His fists gripped my hair, moving it away from my face, and his hips rocked forward, plunging him deeper into my mouth.

'Christ, angel.' He cursed low under his breath and tilted my chin up so I'd meet his eyes. 'You like doing that to me, don't you?' He brushed a knuckle along my cheek and I nodded. 'Does that taste good?' he asked, teasing me.

I smiled wickedly and licked along the head of his cock again, tasting the salty bead of fluid leaking from his tip. His cock twitched and he moaned something unintelligible again.

'Lie back,' he ordered.

I lay down against the pillows, watching him, waiting for him to make his move, but he seemed entirely unrushed and content to just take in my naked form, a slight smile curling at his mouth. For a sex addict, he seemed much too in control, and the thought made me smile. He was mine. All his past troubles and all the worries we'd overcome made this moment that much sweeter, like it meant more because we'd worked to get here.

Knox lay down beside me, covering me with the warm weight of his body, and sank inside me slowly, letting me acclimate to him an inch at a time.

Chapter Ten

Knox

Holy shit, she felt amazing. It took several minutes to work myself completely inside her, but the patience was worth it. My eyes slipped closed the moment I was fully buried inside McKenna's warm heat. She might have been prim and proper outside the bedroom, but my angel liked to get a little dirty between the sheets, further proof that she was the perfect girl for me. I whispered dirty things into her ear as I fucked her slowly—telling her how tight she was around me, how good she felt, and she let out tiny whimpers each time I did.

Everything about her was incredible, and I knew without a doubt that I was a very fucking lucky man. Her pussy was like crack and I kept up an easy tempo, enjoying the feelings flooding through me.

'I can feel you tightening around my cock. Do you want to come?' I asked, letting my lips brush past the shell of her ear.

'Yes,' she said and moaned. The hint of desperation in her voice told me that while I'd been waiting for her, she'd been holding herself back, waiting for me. And since I knew she'd been turned on and wet since our ride home, I wanted to take care of her.

I pressed my thumb against her clit, eliciting a soft cry from her, and began lightly rubbing as I continued the even rhythm of my strokes, pushing in and out of her. McKenna flew apart, convulsing and squirming in my arms, repeating my name over and over again until the last of her orgasm pulsed through her body and left her limp and sated in my arms.

Not yet done with her, I pulled her hips to mine, entering her deeply. Her back arched off the bed at the unexpected invasion. Her eyes had that glassy, faraway look, and I could tell she was undone. I wanted to flip her over, to sink into her from behind and watch her ass wiggle against my thrusts, but I knew I was too close. And McKenna was worn out.

'I'm almost there,' I murmured, kissing her neck.

Pumping into her again and I again, I felt my balls draw up close to my body as her tight muscles gripped me. A shuddering moan pushed past my lips as she milked my cock deep inside her body. 'Kenna…' The broken groan rumbled deep in my chest and I collapsed onto the bed on top of her, gathering her in my arms and holding her tightly against my chest.

As our heartbeats pounded together, I knew I couldn't put off the truth about my past much longer. It wasn't fair to her. She'd given me everything—her heart, her devotion, her virginity, for fuck's sake, and I couldn't even tell her the truth. McKenna had given me a chance at true happiness, and the boys had a loving female in their lives for the first time in years. I was being selfish hiding this from her and it was starting to eat at me, to wear a hole in my newly mended heart. It wasn't fucking healthy.

I held her securely, breathing in the scent of her shampoo as a million thoughts swirled through my brain. She'd healed me, made me a better man, yet none of that could erase my past. I held on to hope that since she'd forgiven me once before, she could find a way to do it again. If only there was a way to show her how sorry I was, she could understand my dark past was truly behind me.

Chapter Eleven

Knox

'Guys, come on, we're going to be late.' I corralled my brothers toward the front door and they groggily obliged, slipping into shoes and coats.

'If this is lunch, why do we have to be up at the crack of dawn?' Jaxon yawned. His face looked a hell of a lot better since the beat down, just the hint of a shadow darkened his left cheekbone.

'Because,' I said. 'There's training beforehand and we need to have everything ready for one hundred fifty people by noon. Come on.'

I'd arranged for us to volunteer at a church today to serve lunch to a Mothers Against Drunk Drivers group that was having an all-day retreat. McKenna was meeting us there later. I knew it was fucked up that I hadn't told her the truth yet about my own past with drunk driving. I guess this was my own twisted way of trying to make amends.

When we arrived at the church, we parked in the back and tramped down the stairs to the basement and into the large kitchen. McKenna was already inside, and a large smile spread across her face when she saw us.

'Hi!' She bounded across the room and flung herself into my arms. 'This was such a good idea.' She kissed me warmly on the mouth. It was more than I deserved and a twinge of guilt flashed through me. *Shit.*

'Hi, angel,' I murmured, pressing a kiss to her forehead.

She greeted each of the boys in a similar fashion, with hugs and kisses on their cheeks. She was so good to them, filling the void left behind when Mom died, that my chest tightened and I had to turn away.

'So, where do we start?' I surveyed the large kitchen.

McKenna had gotten there early and met with the church kitchen staff. We were making lasagna, salad, and brownies, and she gave each of us an apron as she explained the tasks.

Tucker and I teamed up on the brownies, Jaxon was going to make the salad, and McKenna and Luke were going to prepare the main dish. It would take us a couple of hours to prepare the huge batches of food, plus cleanup time afterward.

Putting Tucker on dessert probably wasn't the wisest idea. He kept stealing the pieces of chocolate I was roughly chopping. I glanced over at Jaxon, who was chopping tomatoes into slimy little chunks, and almost chuckled at the disdain on his face. Public service was good for him. Maybe this would get him to open his eyes and see there was more to life than gambling and girls.

McKenna and Luke gathered their ingredients and were beginning to assemble pans of lasagna noodles and sauce.

'You sure you want me to have all that money?' Luke asked her, a questioning look in his eyes. He wasn't any more used to handouts than I was, and that made me proud.

'Of course I'm sure. It would make me very happy to see you off at college. That's the best use of the money I could think of.'

'You're too good to us.' He playfully tossed a noodle in her direction.

McKenna caught it and smiled at him. 'Yeah, well, I kind of have a thing for your brother...'

He laughed. 'Trust me, I noticed.' His expression grew thoughtful for a few moments as he layered cheese over the bed of noodles. 'It's just really cool of you to forgive him.'

'Forgive him?' she questioned, peering up from her task to meet his eyes with an inquisitive expression.

My stomach turned sour and dropped like a stone.

Chapter Twelve

McKenna

Luke and I were elbow deep in noodles and tomato sauce, and I was trying to understand what he meant about me forgiving Knox. I knew Knox's background as a sex addict, but since I'd forgiven that a while ago, something told me there was more Luke was referring to.

Using my clean hand to push a lock of hair behind my ear, I turned to face Luke. 'What do you mean?'

He swallowed and his gaze wandered over to Knox's. Knox looked like someone had punched him in the stomach. His shoulders were rounded forward and his face had gone pale. Knox shook his head at Luke, and his mouth pulled into a frown.

My hands felt shaky and I gripped the edge of the counter for support. 'L-Luke?' I stammered.

The entire kitchen went still and silent as the weight of this moment bore down on us. Something was about to happen. Something Knox didn't want me to know, if his reaction was any indication.

'It's time, Knox. She needs to know. No more hiding, right?' Luke said, his voice barely above a whisper.

I licked my lips and faced Luke again, my eyes begging his for the truth.

Without any further prompting, Luke took a deep breath and began. 'All of this—Knox cleaning up his act, us being here today, volunteering for a drunk-driving cause—it's Knox's way of trying. Listen to me. He loves you. Don't forget that.'

I nodded slowly, fighting to comprehend where this was headed. 'Tell me, Luke.'

Luke's gaze shot over to Knox once again. 'You gonna do this, or should I?'

Knox dropped the knife he'd been holding onto the chopping block. 'I will.'

Escorting me to a back hallway, Knox's fingertips at the small of my back felt cold and lifeless. He was terrified for me to learn whatever he was about to tell me, and I was equally as scared. Just as my life had begun to stabilize, I sensed everything I thought I knew was about to change. The feeling was disorienting.

Knox and I stood in silence for several heartbeats. I was torn between wanting him to tell me the truth about whatever it was he'd been hiding, and living in blissful ignorance for a while longer.

'You know I love you, right?' he started.

I nodded slowly. The sentiment that sometimes love wasn't enough pushed itself to the forefront of my brain, and I steeled myself for whatever he was going to say next.

'You never asked about the reason I showed up at that first sex addicts meeting. And I never offered the information.'

He was right. I didn't know why it never occurred to me before, but now I was filled with curiosity. What had prompted him to take that step? I recalled he'd said that he was there at the request of his counselor. 'You were in counseling,' I offered.

'Yes.'

'Why?' I asked softly. I could only assume it had something to do with sex, and I shuddered at the thought. Had he hurt someone? Done something awful?

'We should talk about this later, when we have more—'

I shook my head. I needed to know. 'I know about your past, what more could you possibly tell me?'

'You don't know everything.' He hung his head.

'You're scaring me. Did you father a child you never told me about?'

'No. But I have a feeling that might be easier for you to stomach.'

'Knox. Just tell me.'

'All right,' he said, running a hand roughly through his hair so it stood in odd directions. 'Promise me one thing. That you won't run.'

I nodded. 'I'm here. You have me.'

Agony twisted his features. 'Before I met you, I was a mess. Weekends were my escape from reality, and I used them to their fullest. I drank too much, fucked too often, and didn't really care about the ramifications.'

I waited for him to continue, the sound of my own heartbeat thundering in my ears.

'One night last summer, I got a little too fucked up. And instead of walking home like I should have, or calling a cab, I drove my Jeep home. Or at least, I tried to.'

My hands clutched at the cement wall behind me, fighting for something solid to hold on to.

'I was pulled over and arrested that night for drunk driving. I had no business being behind the wheel, and I spent that night and most of the next day in jail. My brothers were terrified something horrible had happened to me. I'm all they have, and it was a huge fucking wake-up call that I couldn't abandon them like everyone else had. I knew I could never do something that reckless ever again, but the damage was done. I was convicted of drunk driving, sentenced to community service, and ordered to see a counselor for anger management after smarting off with the judge. The counselor I saw diagnosed me with sexual addiction rather than anger issues, and referred me to SAA.'

I felt betrayed in the deepest way. Knox's past had collided with my own, and the wreckage was overwhelming. 'Why didn't you ever tell me?'

'When I asked you about how you became a sex addiction counselor, I'd wanted to hear about your sordid past, maybe learn that you'd overcome this addiction yourself and turned your struggle into helping others. But instead, you were simply a good person who was stepping in to help. It made me feel like a fucking charity case. I couldn't tell you then. And since I wanted to see where this was headed, I didn't.'

Part of me understood why he didn't open up with that information right away. But later, once we were together and he knew about my parents, there was just no excuse. And now him being here today, volunteering at a drunk-driving charity, it felt like a sorry excuse for an apology. I felt tricked and cheated. The man I'd come to love with my whole heart had hidden part of himself from me.

'Tell me what you're thinking,' he said, his voice whisper soft.

'I'm going to need some time.'

Knox nodded, acknowledging my need for space and time to sort through the conflicting feelings inside me. I hated drunk drivers, despising the reckless, careless attitude that put them behind the wheel and endangered others. And I'd just learned the man I loved was one of them, and not only that, but he'd hidden it from me for months.

Tears streamed down my cheeks. 'I need to go…'

He nodded. 'Okay. I'll tell the boys you had to leave. Just don't give up on me, McKenna.'

''Bye, Knox.'

Knox

In the moments before I told McKenna, her blind faith in me made it all the more painful. She'd watched me with those wide blue eyes, waiting for whatever I was about to say. And I knew

77

it was going to fucking crush her. There was nothing worse than the feeling of hurting her. She was so sweet, so pure. She didn't deserve the shit I put her through.

My troubles with the law—my court-appointed counseling sessions, the entire reason I'd met her—all of it stemmed from drunk driving. I'd just completely shattered her world. And I hated the sight of her face going completely pale as all the blood drained away. It wasn't fair asking her not to run. Of course she was going to run. I was a monster of the worst kind. I couldn't even be honest with the woman who owned the deepest part of me.

I headed back into the kitchen in a daze to face my brothers.

'What happened?' Jaxon asked, concern lacing his features.

'She's gone, isn't she?' Luke asked.

I nodded, confirming the worst. It was what I'd expected, but it stung more than I thought it would. The urge to hit something flared inside me. My hands curled into fists as I tried to calm the deep, searing anger burning inside me. I'd found the perfect girl—given her my heart—and it was all for nothing. Maybe this was punishment for all the girls I'd used and tossed aside over the years. Karma was a motherfucking bitch.

And now I needed to put on my happy face and be there for my brothers. Our little adventure today suddenly seemed so trite—we were fucking volunteering at a drunk-driving benefit. How in the world I ever thought this could make up for my lack of honesty with the girl I loved, I had no idea.

'Knox?' Tucker's little voice broke my concentration from the spot I'd been studying on the floor. His brown eyes were flooded with worry.

'Everything's gonna be okay, bud. I promise.'

I had no fucking clue if that was true, but I couldn't admit that to him. If it wasn't true, if she couldn't forgive me, I was going to head into the nearest bar for liquor and pussy to numb myself with.

Chapter Thirteen

McKenna

I was in love with a man I could never be with. We'd success-fully hurdled his sexual addiction and that was the easy part. But this...I had no words. I never dreamed our shared, shattered pasts would be what stood in our way. We'd come too far. Lost too much. The universe was playing some sick joke on me, seeing just how far I could be pushed before I snapped. Well, this was it. I'd reached my breaking point. The score was the universe: one, McKenna: zero.

Knox hiding this from me the entire time hurt worse than finding out he'd been convicted of the crime in the first place. The very crime that killed my parents. My life was rocky enough. I needed a man who was capable of complete honesty, someone to build a stable foundation with. Someone I could trust and rely on. I couldn't share my life with someone with dark secrets, living in constant fear of what he'd reveal next. Because something told me if I knew all the ways Knox had messed up, I'd run away screaming, no matter how big my heart was.

But of course it wasn't that easy. I loved him. I couldn't just turn that off. And there were the boys to think about, too, sweet Tucker and Luke, and heaven knew Jaxon could use a positive role model. I hated the idea of just disappearing from their lives.

Two long and hard days had passed since Knox told me. And now that I knew the full extent of his past, the decision was mine. Either forgive him and let it go, and move forward with our future, or let it destroy everything we'd built.

Through my work at the teen center, I'd counseled woman and girls who were codependent, who felt worthless and rejected without a man in their lives. Women who were depressed and even suicidal over their relationship status. I never in my wildest dreams thought I could be like those women. I had listened to their troubles, asked all the right questions, probed gently and offered the advice I'd learned to give them in my training, yet I felt emotionless and detached from their problems. I was just doing my job.

It was only now that I finally understood. Only since Knox had invaded my life and taken over my every waking thought. Sex and love had the ability to consume you, and it terrified me. I felt desperate and needy and wanted him to love me, to draw me into his arms and never let me go. I didn't know how I could ever look those sad women in the eye again and tell them to move on. There was no moving on. Not once you'd met your true match. Something told me Knox had left an imprint on my heart, in my psyche, that would forever be there.

There was no choice. I had to find a way to move past this. Not that I wasn't furious at him for hiding the truth from me for all these months—I was. It was going to take some time for me to adjust to that. But I knew I would forgive him. How could I not? My love for him was too desperate, too all-consuming for us to be apart. Despite all his mistakes and dark secrets, I loved that man with my whole being. It wasn't a choice.

Gathering up my courage, I texted Knox and asked him to come over and talk. I felt safer having this conversation in my own space. Plus when Amanda had called earlier and asked if I wanted to come over and help out with the baby, Brian had volunteered to go in my place, leaving me alone in the apartment.

Knox confirmed he would be here as soon as he'd fed the boys dinner. I used the time to tidy up my room, too restless and on edge to sit and relax.

When the doorbell to my apartment buzzed a short time later, I nearly jumped out of my skin with the anticipation of seeing him again. I knew that no matter what happened, tonight would be big for me. I had worked on forgiving myself, moving past my parents' tragic deaths, and now it seemed that God had a sense of humor because I was being tested for a final time with forgiving Knox.

His somber expression greeted me when I opened the door. Dark circles lined his eyes as if he hadn't slept, and his hair was messy, standing up in several directions.

'Come inside.' I motioned him forward into the foyer, thankful that Brian was gone to help out with Amanda yet again. He'd been so helpful over the last few days, driving her and the baby to their doctors' checkups and to the store for more diapers.

I led Knox into the living room, but we were both too tense to sit down. The mood surrounding us was sobering. I'd never seen Knox look so broken and defeated. Not even when Jaxon had been beaten and threatened by that gang.

Knox shoved his hands into his pockets and looked up at me through dark lashes. 'There's no excuse for what I did. And not telling you earlier was—'

'I know,' I offered. I could see the sincerity and regret written all over him.

'I'm sorry,' he said simply.

'I know,' I said again. His features were twisted in agony, and even though I'd decided to forgive him and move past it, he didn't know that yet. I decided to use that to my advantage. 'Where did you see this headed? You and me?'

Pressing his fingertips to his temples, he briefly closed his eyes and then opened them again, fixing me with a desperate stare. 'I love you like I've never loved anyone. I wanted you to move in, to be with me forever. I wanted to marry you, angel.'

His admission completely stunned me, and I stood there motionless trying to process his words. I knew Knox wanted me to move in with him, something we hadn't even fully discussed, but now he was telling me that he wanted to marry me, too. My heart swelled three times its normal size in my chest and I briefly closed my eyes.

I struggled to put into words all the emotions I was feeling. But I knew I couldn't answer him now. 'I need time to think, Knox.'

He nodded. 'I get that. Completely.' He stepped closer, closing the distance between us, and tipped my chin up to his. 'But don't forget that you're the one who taught me about vulnerability and letting others in. I know I'm damaged goods, angel, and that this is a huge leap of faith for you...but please believe me when I tell you I love you. All of you. And I always will.'

I nodded. I did believe that. Knox was a changed man, inside and out. He was my everything. He and his family had become my whole world, and I loved each and every one of them. I just needed some time to clear the thoughts swirling in my head and do this my way.

'We'll talk soon,' was all I said.

I knew Knox would be mad that Brian was the one taking me to get my first car, but I also knew he'd understand. As long as I got something safe and reliable and wasn't depending on public transit anymore, he'd let it go. Besides, I wanted to do this for myself, and inviting my oldest friend along felt like the right thing to do. Especially since I needed to tell him something big, something that would forever change the dynamic of our relationship.

I hadn't spoken to Knox since he came to my apartment several days ago. And even though I missed him with every ounce of my being, it felt good taking control of my life and getting things in order. I'd put that off for far too long.

Brian and I toured the car lot, and I selected a slightly used silver sedan to test drive. Once the salesman had made a photocopy of my driver's license, Brian and I were seated in the air-freshener-scented interior, ready to take a spin.

Gripping the wheel at ten and two, I waited for a large break in the traffic and pulled out onto the road. 'So you've been seeing more of Amanda these days,' I said as I drove. It wasn't a question, and Brian merely glanced up at me without responding. 'That's a good thing, right?'

He nodded, a smile barely visible on his lips. Good thing I knew him so well.

'How is she doing?' I asked.

'She's great. She's an incredible mom. It's a big burden being a single parent, but I've never heard her complain once.'

'You like her.'

He chuckled at me. 'I do. She's a sweet girl.'

'What about the fact that she has a baby. Does that scare you?'

He looked thoughtful for a moment, but shook his head. 'Not at all.'

It was the same way I felt about Knox having custody of his three brothers. If anything, the responsibility only deepened him and enriched our relationship. There was a whole other side of him to love. They were never a burden. Well, except when we wanted alone time, but I was getting distracted. 'So are you guys, like, dating?'

Brian nodded. 'Yeah, I think so. We haven't technically been on any dates yet. She has a three-week-old daughter, you know? But I bring her dinner, we watch movies, and I really don't mind pitching in to take care of AnnMarie. She's a good baby.'

'You're a good guy, Brian.' I felt proud of my friend. He was growing up and moving on, just like I was. 'I think I'm going to get this car.'

'It's a great car for the money and seems to run well.'

I nodded. I hadn't brought him with me to talk about cars or Amanda, so I gathered my courage for what was really on my mind. 'Bri?'

'Hmm?' he asked, gazing out the passenger window.

'Knox has asked me to live with him.'

I felt his gaze turn toward me, but like the chicken I was, I continued staring out the front windshield.

'Oh yeah?' he asked.

I nodded. 'Yeah. And I've decided to move in with him.'

'Wow. That's a big step, McKenna. Are you sure you guys are—'

'I'm sure. He's my everything.'

'I get it. I could tell from the first time I met him that there was something major between you two.'

It was nice to hear him acknowledge that. He understood that Knox and I were a package deal.

We sat in silence for the duration of the trip back to the dealership, and I wondered what he was really thinking about all this. When I pulled back into the parking lot and went inside to sign the paperwork, Brian lingered on the car lot. I watched him through the showroom windows, walking around to look at the new cars, and unease churned inside me. He wasn't going to make some last desperate plea for me, was he?

Finally I met him outside with my new car keys and found him lingering beside his car.

'Hey,' he said.

'Hey.'

'Get it all squared away?'

I raised the keys in my hand and gave them a jingle. 'You're looking at the proud new owner of a Volkswagen Jetta.' I grinned.

'Good for you.' He returned my smile, but the worry line creasing his forehead was still present.

'Brian, what's…'

'McKenna, listen…'

We both paused, laughing at the other.

'You go first,' I said. I braced myself for whatever it was that he was going to say. I was strong enough to handle it. Even if he tried to tell me that my parents wouldn't have approved of Knox, I was certain that wasn't true. They would be proud of any man who stepped up to raise his family and took good care of me, too.

'Amanda's living situation isn't ideal. She has two roommates, plus her and the baby in a small apartment. She and AnnMarie share a room, and I was thinking…' Brian paused and earnest blue eyes met mine. 'I know it's sudden and not like me, but with you moving out, I'd like to ask Amanda to move in with me. We can set up your bedroom as a nursery for the baby. There'll be more room for toys and all the gear that comes with a baby, and I really like Amanda. Like, I really, *really* like her. I want to make this work.'

His admission stunned me. I had no idea he liked Amanda so much. But honestly, I should have pieced it together. He'd been at her apartment almost every day since I'd introduced them at the hospital, and he'd come home with a big dopey grin on his face each time. It crossed my mind that Brian might not know about her past with sex addiction, but I knew that was a conversation he and Amanda needed to have. It wasn't my place.

'I think that's amazing news.' I pulled him in for a hug. 'Have you asked her yet?'

'No. Not yet. I've been thinking about asking her about getting our own place, but I didn't want to just leave you behind. Now that I know you're moving in with Knox…it just makes sense. It feels right, you know?'

Something told me Amanda would say yes. She'd texted me a couple of times mentioning how sweet my roommate was. She was falling for him, too. 'Go tell her. I'm going to head over to Knox's place.'

Brian nodded. 'Okay. I think I'm gonna stop on the way and pick up a gift for AnnMarie. What do you get for a three-week-old baby?' he asked.

'Diapers?'

He chuckled. 'You're probably right.'

As he turned for his car, my hand on his forearm stopped him. 'Bri...thanks for everything.'

His eyes met mine. 'Anytime. You know I'm always here for you. I'm always going to be here, no matter where we live or who is in our lives.'

I nodded. I did. And it was a comforting feeling. 'Text me later and tell me what she says.'

'Will do. Have fun with the boys.'

I hadn't told Brian about my fight with Knox, or his drunk-driving arrest. I merely nodded. But inside, my stomach was coiled tight. It was time to go face the music.

Chapter Fourteen

McKenna

A few hours later, I showed up on Knox's doorstep with a duffel bag slung over my shoulder, wondering what I'd find on the other side of the door. Could he have given up on me already and moved on? It was too painful to think about. I had to believe, with blind faith, that this would all work. I was out of options. Knox and I hadn't spoken in a couple of days, not since I told him I needed my space. But now that I'd told Brian he could move Amanda and the baby into my old room, I was out of choices. This had to work.

Just like he did the first time I came to this house, Tucker answered the door. 'Kenna!' he shouted and flung himself into my arms. It immediately made me feel guilty about staying away for so long.

'Hey, buddy.' I ruffled his hair and glanced around. Jaxon and Luke were in the living room, staring at a game of basketball on TV. Knox was nowhere to be seen, and dread churned deep inside me. 'Where's Knox?' I asked, my voice coming out shakier than I intended it to.

Throwing an arm around my waist, Tucker led me inside. 'He's working right now, but can you stay over and hang out with me?' Big brown eyes blinked up at mine. He was impossible to say no to. Just like his big brother.

'Of course I'll stay.' I set my bag down in the living room and joined the boys on the couch.

Luke and Jaxon both nodded their hellos, not bothering to break eye contact with the TV until halftime. But I supposed if I was going to be living here, all of this was going to be my life. Boys, boys, and more boys. I nearly giggled at the thought.

'Do you know when Knox gets off work?' I asked.

Luke's dark, expressive eyes met mine and I knew he was remembering the volunteer event where he'd practically forced Knox's hand at telling me the truth. Luke had taken a risk, and I appreciated his honesty. His heart was in the right place. I hoped my small smile conveyed my thanks.

'He's closing up at the hardware store, it should be about another hour.'

I caught up with the boys. Jaxon had cut out gambling, Luke was waiting to hear about the college applications he'd submitted, and Tucker was just Tucker. Loud, animated, and excitable like an eight-year-old boy should be. Thankfully, with Tucker to entertain me, the minutes passed by quickly.

'Have you guys had dinner yet?'

'Nope,' they chimed in unison.

Unable to sit and wait any longer, I ventured into the kitchen to see what I could make for dinner. The cabinets and fridge were pretty much bare, but I pieced together bread and cheese for grilled cheese sandwiches and a couple of cans of soup. I hope Knox wasn't expecting a gourmet chef with me moving in. But I somehow knew he wouldn't be. The guys had been taking care of themselves for many years already. They wouldn't expect me to fill the role of maid or cook; I could just be me. The thought made me smile. The soup bubbled away on the stove and I added the last of the sandwiches to a big platter, carrying the whole thing out to the dining table.

'Boys, dinner!' I called.

I realized the extra commotion I heard from the living room meant Knox had arrived home. My stomach somersaulted and suddenly food was the last thing on my mind.

Knox entered the kitchen and his weary expression found mine. 'McKenna?'

'Hi.'

'What are you...'

'I made dinner.'

His gaze ventured to the table. 'I see that.'

'Boys, come and eat up while it's still hot. I'm just going to talk to Knox,' I instructed them. It was all the encouragement they needed. They descended on the food like a pack of hungry wolves.

'Guys, save some for McKenna,' Knox said before shooting me an apologetic look.

We headed into the kitchen while the guys busied themselves with the food I'd made in the dining room.

'Sorry about them. You'd think they've never seen food before,' he joked.

I smiled. 'It's okay.'

'What's going on, angel? I take you didn't come here just to make dinner.'

'No. I didn't. I'm here because you were right. Your past was hard for me to accept, but it's also the thing that led you straight to me, and I can't help but think it was fate or maybe some divine intervention.'

His forehead creased and he took a step closer, obviously trying to understand what I was telling him.

I took a deep breath and continued. 'The exact thing I was running from led me to Chicago and pushed you straight into my path. I'm not going to lie and say this isn't hard for me. It's the hardest test I've ever had to overcome. Harder than coping with life without my parents. Harder than leaving my hometown behind. But loving you isn't a choice. And it's worth it, Knox. You're everything to me. You, your brothers, this home and family you're offering me. I want it. I want all of it. I won't allow my past to rob me of any more joy. You messed up, but you've changed. You're not the same man who got behind that wheel. And I understand the life circumstances that drove you down that path. I know there will be bumps and bruises as we figure this out together. But I'm not going anywhere. You have me. You've had my heart right from the beginning.'

Without a word, Knox gathered me in his arms, tugging me to his chest and lifting my feet from the floor. I buried my nose in the crook between his neck and his shoulder and inhaled the scent I'd missed so much. 'God, it feels good to hold you, to have you back,' he said.

'You have me. And I'm planning on staying if you still want me here.'

He pulled back to meet my eyes, still holding me so my feet didn't reach the floor. 'For good?'

I nodded, a big dopey grin overtaking my mouth.

'I don't know how I could possibly deserve you, but I love you, McKenna.'

'I love you,' I returned, 'and your entire rowdy family.' We could hear the boys arguing over how to divide up the food in the other room.

He grinned down at me and kissed my forehead. 'Should we go tell the boys?'

I nodded.

Back inside the dining room, I saw that the entire plate of sandwiches was gone except for stray pieces of crust, and only about an inch of soup remained in the pot. I guess I'd underestimated the appetites of three growing boys. I'd have to remember that next time I made them dinner.

'Guys, I have some news.' Knox's hand found mine and he linked our fingers together, tugging me closer. 'I asked McKenna to live with us and she said yes.'

Luke's face immediately broke into a wide grin and all three of them looked surprised, but happy. I wondered if they'd ask deeper questions, like what this meant for the relationship between Knox and me, or logistical ones, like how we would divvy up bathroom time and share household chores. But the room remained completely silent and still.

Until Tucker passed gas.

Loudly.

Okay, so apparently they're comfortable around me.

Everyone broke into fits of laughter, me included.

'I think you should consider yourself christened. Welcome to the family,' Jaxon said.

'Rule numero uno, no farting at the dinner table, dude.' Luke frowned at Tucker, who in turn stuck out his tongue.

'On that note, should we go upstairs?' Knox asked.

I nodded, not wanting to stick around and experience the smell that had already caused Jaxon and Luke to run for cover while Tucker laughed hysterically.

'I will feed you, but first I just need to be alone with you,' Knox whispered near my ear as we started up the stairs.

I wondered what he had in mind for this alone time.

'What do you want for dinner?' he asked, once we were all alone in his bedroom. Our bedroom. I wondered if *cock* would be the wrong answer. My recovering sex-addict boyfriend was turning me into a raging sex addict. And I liked it.

'I'm not really hungry for food just yet.' I met his deep brown gaze and bit my lower lip. I had no idea if my sexy stare was appealing, but the low growl that rumbled in his chest and the way he stalked toward me caused my stomach to coil into a tight knot. I wanted him. I wanted everything—our future—all the pleasure he could give me, and I couldn't wait another second.

Knox

I had a new addiction: loving McKenna. The fact that she was here at all, let alone telling me that she still wanted to be with me was amazing, and that she was moving in…well, she continually blew my mind with her willingness to forgive. She inspired me in so many ways. There would be no going back to that lost and broken man I was before her. I believed what she said was true. We were brought into each other's lives at just the right moment.

McKenna secured her hands around the back of my neck, her fingers curling into my hair. I lowered my mouth to kiss her sweet lips, but held part of myself back. Sex wasn't the right way to show her how I felt about her, but in that moment, I didn't think she cared. She rubbed herself wantonly against my groin, causing my dick to harden, which wasn't abnormal around her. My cock had been in a semierect state since the day I met her. She'd become my everything. There was no turning back now.

I'd lived without the gentle, loving touch of a woman for so long, though, that I wasn't about to stop McKenna. Her fingers continued toying with my hair while our mouths moved together.

I'd loved my mother so much. I wasn't afraid to admit it. I was a momma's boy growing up. Losing her took a piece of me that I wouldn't get back, a piece that no woman could ever replace, no matter how hard I'd tried. And trust me, I'd tried. I fell into bed with girl after girl, looking for some kind of connection. But since my hardened heart believed that love only ended in pain, I never got my happy ending. It was something I thought I'd live without. Until I met McKenna. I had to love and forgive myself before I could open myself up to another. Opening my zipper wasn't enough. I knew McKenna would give me some line about how it was normal, how sex addicts substituted sexual experiences for emotional intimacy, but it all finally clicked.

'Knox…' She breathed out my name, then inhaled against my neck. A jolt of desire shot straight to my groin, hardening me the rest of the way.

'Yeah, angel?'

Her hands found the tense bulge below my belt and she gave him a gentle squeeze. 'Don't make me beg.'

Christ, how could I say no to that? Big blue eyes met mine, urging me on, making me want to give her whatever she asked for.

'I need to say a few things first.' I fought to control my pounding heartbeat that I could feel pulsing in my cock. *Damn.*

McKenna waited, blinking up at me silently. God, she was beautiful. I didn't think I'd ever get used to her natural beauty—to her blue eyes that showed her every thought and emotion, to the soft curves that swayed when she walked, to her too-big heart that caused her to take care of everything and everyone in her path.

Taking her left hand, I guided her to my bed, lowering us both onto the edge. I stroked her naked ring finger, dreaming about the day I'd make her mine. I wanted to be the one to tuck her into bed each night, the first one to see her sleepy smile in the morning, the only man to listen to the gentle sounds of her breathing as she fell into a deep sleep. I wanted to be the only man to make love to her. And I told her all that and more, the words rushing out from me as I watched her eyes grow teary.

'Shhh, don't cry. Just tell me you want all that, too.'

She nodded, her misty blue eyes looking happy despite the tears. Using my thumbs, I brushed the dampness from her cheeks.

'Will you marry me, angel?'

McKenna's voice broke in a tiny whisper and she flung her arms around my neck, repeating the word *yes* again and again. Never had one little word sounded so good.

I felt like pumping my fist in the air, but settled for squeezing her tight in my arms and peppering her neck with kisses while she continued to sob quietly. Actually, I wasn't sure if it was crying or laughing since her mouth was curled up in a pretty smile.

'Say something, baby. Is this too fast for you?'

She shook her head. 'It's perfect, Knox. I want to be with you always.' A crease pinched her brow.

'What is it?'

'I just…I don't want a big wedding. With my parents gone…'

I understood completely. Big events and holidays were hard without a family around you to celebrate with. But I knew we would make new traditions as the years passed. 'Whatever you want.'

'Maybe just the courthouse—with the boys there, too.'

'Whatever you want,' I promised again. 'But you will wear a pretty dress for me, and we will celebrate.'

She nodded, her smile blossoming wider.

Knowing I couldn't stave off my raw need for her any longer, I pressed her back against the mattress, bringing my mouth to hers in a searing kiss.

Removing her clothing piece by piece, I trailed my mouth down her body, licking and biting her succulent flesh. My teeth grazed her rib cage, earning me a tiny shriek as I moved lower, leaving damp, sucking kisses along her belly. McKenna squirmed, her hips undulating, and her chest rising and falling rapidly. Pushing her panties to the side, I swept my finger along her silken center, earning me a small whimper of pleasure. My own groan of satisfaction followed. I loved making her feel good. She didn't even have to touch me. Well, that wasn't entirely true. If I didn't come soon I'd probably have a massive case of blue balls later.

'You want me to kiss this sweet pussy?' I murmured, my lips just millimeters from her smooth core.

A helpless groan and her fist in my hair were apparently the only responses I was getting. I pressed an innocent kiss against her pussy lips, before spreading her apart so I could run my tongue along the length of her. Her fist tightened in my hair, holding me right where she wanted me. With my mouth curling into a smile, my tongue found her clit and I licked her over and over, timing my tempo to the sounds of her moans. It was easy to read just what she liked.

When she was close, I pushed my index finger inside her, pressing against the spot deep inside on her front wall, and I felt her body contract as she started to come. Adding my middle finger, I continued fucking her with my hand while my mouth latched onto a nipple. 'You like when I kiss your sexy tits, huh, baby?' She rode my fingers, pumping her hips as her eyes locked onto mine.

The force of McKenna's orgasm caused her to clench around my fingers and cry out in bliss. Fuck, I needed to think about soundproofing my bedroom. I loved how hard I could make her come, though. Watching her cheeks and neck color with blush as the blood rushed to the surface of her skin was a huge turn-on. I loved the effect I had on her.

Stripping myself of my clothes in three seconds flat, I gripped my eager cock, stroking it slowly and moved alongside her. 'I need to be inside you so bad.'

'Yes…' she said and groaned.

Her pussy was still hypersensitive from her orgasm, and not to mention incredibly tight as I tried to penetrate her. 'Relax for me, baby,' I reminded her. McKenna drew a deep breath and worked at relaxing her muscles, allowing me to slip inside several more inches. She felt like a hot molten fist squeezing me. It was a testament to my control that I didn't immediately come.

Tensing my muscles and clenching my ass, I pumped into her hard and fast. The next time I would go slow, but I needed to spill myself inside her. I couldn't explain it, not even to myself. But I needed to give in to this raw, primal connection we had to show myself it was more than sex. I loved her and I knew she felt it, regardless of whether the sex was sweet and slow or hard and fast.

I met her eyes and kissed her again, unwilling to break our connection in any way. With her blue eyes on mine, her tongue lightly stroking my bottom lip, and my cock buried deep inside her, I found the meaning and connection I'd been looking for all along. Sex with the woman I loved was better than I ever could have imagined.

Forcing myself to slow, if only to draw out her pleasure and mine, I felt her begin to contract around me again. I dragged my cock in and out slowly, grinding my groin against hers to put pressure directly on her clit. Her tight little pussy clamped down hard around me as she climaxed. *Fuck it.* I was going to come.

My own release hit me like a punch to the gut and I cried out her name, burying my face against her neck as I spilled myself inside her.

McKenna's phone chimed from the bedside table and she reached for it, checking her text messages. The sheet dropped away from her chest, and though we'd already gone twice, my body didn't fail to notice her luscious curves.

'Who is it?' I asked, trailing a hand along the curve of her spine.

'Brian.' She grinned.

'I just gave you three orgasms and you're smiling about a text from Brian?'

She frowned and slugged me on the shoulder. 'Hush. You and I both know there's not a thing wrong with your ego.'

She had me there. I knew how to make my girl insane with desire.

'Amanda said yes,' she continued. 'She's moving in with him.'

'Wow. Those two? Really?'

She nodded. 'They hit it off. And I guess when you know, you know.'

'Believe me, *I know*.' I smirked and gave her butt a playful swat. We'd had a bumpy ride, but I knew that would only make us appreciate the good times more. And something told me there were lots of good times in store for us.

McKenna was my addiction.

But somehow I knew that was an addiction she'd approve of. All-consuming need coursed through me and I hauled her over top of me.

'Again?' she asked, her voice rising in surprise to see I was already hard for her again.

'Never question my cock's stamina when it comes to you, angel.' I nudged at her wet opening and a soft, whispery whine was her only response. 'Not too sore, are you?'

'Not yet.'

I sank inside her slowly, knowing she was all I'd ever need.

Epilogue

Two years later

McKenna

'See you tonight, buddy.' I kissed Tucker on the cheek and then watched him board the big yellow school bus waiting at the curb. I stood there for a moment too long, watching him pull away and enjoying the feel of the sun sinking into my pores.

It had been a long winter, made longer by the fact that Jaxon had been in jail for dealing drugs for the past several months. He'd been released last week and had spent the time at home with us, rediscovering himself and preparing for a new life—one away from drugs and gambling and girls. He would spend the summer at a rehabilitation ranch, working and learning to live as a better man.

Knox had been quiet and withdrawn when Jaxon had left. It had taken me some time to get through to him, to get him to see that we were all responsible for our own choices, and that Jaxon was going to make things right. I also had to remind him that we had a lot to be thankful for, the least of which were Luke's achievements at college. He was doing phenomenally well. That seemed to soothe Knox. But I knew it wasn't easy for him being the head of this household. He loved without regard, worried from time to time, and was fiercely protective. It was just one more thing to love about him.

I headed back inside, giddy at the thought that Knox and I were both off work today while Tucker was at school. One thing I never counted on since moving in two years ago was the lack of true alone time. I could count on one hand the number of times when Knox and I had the house all to ourselves.

I found him in the kitchen, sipping orange juice straight from the carton. I shook my head and made a tsking sound. Try as I might, there were just some habits I'd never break these boys of.

'Hey, Mama,' Knox said, stuffing the carton back into the fridge as if I hadn't just witnessed his violation of it.

I giggled at the nickname. Tucker had started calling me Mama Kenna shortly after I moved in and Knox, who thought it was adorable, often used the nickname too, since he knew it always brought a smile to my lips.

'Did you get that boy off to school?' He leaned back against the counter, letting me take in my fill of his naked torso.

Momentarily distracted by the ridiculous six-pack staring back at me, it took me a moment to answer. 'Uh-huh,' I managed.

Knox grinned at my reaction. 'Over two years later and I still get her weak in the knees.'

'Do not!' I couldn't let him know how easily he got me worked up. I didn't want that knowledge going to his head. He already knew he was a complete sex god with command over my body, heart, and soul. Jeez, a girl needed to keep a few secrets.

He pushed off the counter and stalked closer. 'What do you want to do today?' His gaze wandered down my body while his fingertips grazed my hip bone. A zing of electricity darted through my center.

Damn it. There was no denying I wanted him. I shrugged, trying to play it cool. 'I don't know. I was thinking of going to the mall, getting some summer shopping done for me and Tucker. He won't fit into any of his shorts or T-shirts from last year…'

Knox's gaze locked on mine and his fingers tightened as they curled around my hip. 'You have exactly three seconds flat to get this fine little ass up those stairs and undressed,' he growled. 'One...'

I swallowed heavily and met his intense gaze, loving this dangerous game I was playing with him.

'Two...'

I darted around him, but not before I felt the sting of his palm connect with my butt, and jogged for the stairs.

Knox

McKenna was breathless and fighting to push her jeans down her thighs when I entered our room. I struggled to keep the smile off my face as I watched her. My angel liked being told what to do in the bedroom; she loved it when I took charge. Which was good because I loved it, too.

Once she was stripped down to just a pair of blue cotton panties, McKenna stood in front of me. Her jog up the stairs had winded her, and her tits were rising and falling deliciously with each breath she drew. I approached and carefully circled one sensitive nipple with the pad of my index finger, rubbing the soft pink center until it pebbled under my touch.

'Do you want my mouth here?' I continued rubbing and circling her nipples. Her breath hitched in her throat and she murmured some unintelligible sound. I knew that kissing and sucking on her tits got her nice and wet for me, and I couldn't help teasing her.

Lowering my mouth to her chest, I pressed a tiny kiss to the tip of each breast, her skin erupting in chill bumps in the wake of my breath. 'Why are these still on?' Working my fingers into the side of her panties, my fingers found her warm center. Slick and wet, just like I predicted.

I pushed the fabric down her legs until the panties pooled at her ankles and she stepped out of them. Running my fingers along her bare folds, I found her clit and lightly rubbed. McKenna's knees trembled and she reached a steadying hand toward me, grasping my bicep as I continued my assault.

Then I bent to her ear and whispered, 'Get on your knees, angel.'

I took her hand and helped her lower herself to her knees, then unbuttoned and unzipped my jeans, tugging them down just enough to free my cock. It greeted McKenna, begging for her mouth.

Taking the base of me in one hand, she guided me to her mouth. Big blue eyes met mine as she sucked against the head of my cock. *Holy fuck.* Watching her suck my dick was almost as good as the sensation itself. She might not have had experience before, but her passion for me and for this came through loud and clear. She devoured me, pushing as much of my length as she could fit into her mouth, salivating around me and pumping her fist up and down while her other hand cupped my balls. I was hers. She was the only girl who could make me come in about three minutes flat just by sucking me.

I tipped her chin up to mine and her eyes latched on again. 'What do you think you're doing?' I growled, my voice rough with desire.

Considering her mouth was currently full of my cock, she didn't answer, but her eyes implored mine.

'You're a greedy little thing this morning. Why would you try to make me come in your mouth when you know I want to be inside you when I go off?'

She swallowed and the sensation cut straight to my balls where I had to fight off a moan.

'Get on the bed.'

McKenna rose and scrambled up to the bed, lying down on her back and widening her thighs so I could see her pretty pink folds.

Shit, that was a beautiful sight. I drew a couple of deep breaths to calm myself down, or this was going to be over in a damn hurry. Needing a moment to recover, I took my time licking and kissing a trail along her body, spending extra time nibbling the creamy flesh at her inner thighs until she was writhing and groaning beneath me. I flicked my tongue against her clit, bringing her right to the edge of her orgasm before placing a chaste kiss against her pussy and crawling up her body.

When she let out a groan of frustration, I said, 'Same thing you did to me, angel. Fair's fair.' The truth was, there was no way she was coming without me inside her. I needed to feel her tight walls clench around me when she came. I fucking craved it.

As I positioned myself against her and eased inside slowly, my eyes slipped closed and I went to my happy place. The place where I felt content and loved and accepted. McKenna wrapped her legs around my back, tilting her pelvis to meet mine, allowing me to thrust deeper. She could now handle all of me, which sent my cock to his happy place, too.

Dragging my length in and out of her, I cradled her face in my hands and kissed her full mouth, telling her I loved her over and over again.

Knowing that this beautiful girl loved me for the man I was, it made our relationship and our intimate connection that much stronger. We hadn't gotten around to making it official yet, but it was just a matter of time. Maybe this summer on the beach.

'Knox, I'm close...' she murmured, tightening her vice-like grip on my dick.

Fuck.

McKenna let out a short cry and her fingernails bit into my ass as she pressed me closer. I drew out her orgasm, kissing her mouth, her neck, and her breasts as she clung to me, her pussy throbbing deep inside.

I shuddered once and started to come, hot jets of semen pumping out of me and into McKenna as our bodies fought to get even closer together.

Afterward, we laid tangled together in the sheets, our skin dewy from exertion and our hearts still beating too fast. We made plans for the rest of our day together—going out to lunch, and then down to the lake to walk along the beach. I smiled at the secret knowledge that sex one more time before Tucker got home from school would probably be on the agenda, too.

I tugged her closer, drawing her to my chest, thankful that I had at least a million more days like this to look forward to. Before McKenna, I thought I was incapable of love—and maybe I was. But she'd changed something fundamental inside me just by her presence in my life. Her sweet and giving nature, her big heart that had plenty of room for not only me, but also my brothers, and her ability to forgive were all things I loved about her. And I made sure to tell her every day. Now that I'd found her, I would do everything in my control to show her she was the love of my life.

Curling into my side, McKenna released a happy little sigh. Knowing that she felt the exact same way was something indescribable. I felt a deeper connection to her than any other person in the world. She was my everything.